MY BEST MEMORY

HELENE'S STORY

CAROLE WOLFE

BLIND VISTA PRESS

Copyright 2021 Carole Wolfe

All rights reserved.

www.carolewolfe.com

First Edition

ISBN 978-0-9993582-8-3 (eBook)
ISBN 978-0-9993582-9-0 (Paperback)
ISBN 978-1-7371985-0-5 (Large print paperback)

This is a work of fiction. Names, characters, businesses, places, events, locals, and incidents are either the products of the author's imagination or used in a fictitious manner. Any resemblance to actual person, living or dead, or actual events is purely coincidental.

❦ Created with Vellum

1

Helene smoothed a wrinkle from her cream linen pants. She'd have to talk to the dry cleaner again. The quality of his work declined every few months, so it was about time she reminded him of her standards. Tucking a strand of her highlighted hair behind her ear, Helene wished for the thousandth time that she lived in a town with more than one dry cleaner. If she were anywhere but itty-bitty Glen Valley, she could threaten to take her business elsewhere. She still could, but it wasn't convenient. Who wanted to drive forty-five minutes to pick up dry cleaning?

Her husband shifted in the chair next to her, and she glanced at him. Her usually animated and jovial spouse was still mad at her. Helene sighed. Ever since their daughter, Sara, had moved to Chicago, Max remained cold and aloof.

Which was why they were sitting in the office of Priscilla Austen, *Marriage and Family Therapist*. Helene stopped herself from rolling her eyes. She'd noticed the therapist watching them since they'd sat down fifteen minutes prior.

What a waste of time and money, thought Helene as she crossed her ankles. *I can't believe I cancelled my manicure for this.*

If Max thinks I'm going to be the one to start the conversation, he is sorely mistaken.

As if her husband could read her mind, Max turned toward her.

"We aren't leaving here until you talk to Dr. Austen."

"Max, you know you're welcome to call me Priscilla."

Helene smirked. When she'd agreed to attend marriage counseling, she didn't know the therapist would be the same age as their daughters. How could someone with no life experience help them? Helene wondered if this was just a plan to steal Max from her. Memories of other women who thought they could cause problems between them came to mind, but she refused to dwell on them. Max was her husband and always would be.

Maybe. If she could get through this stupid therapy session.

"Dr. Austen." Helene nodded again, refusing to treat this woman with any familiarity. She watched television. She knew how these shrinks manipulated people. Best to keep things as formal as possible. "I'd be happy to talk, but you haven't asked any questions."

Max grunted. "Helene, the first thing Priscilla asked when we walked in was if you knew why you were here. You said because I made you come. When you agreed to therapy, that should have meant you agreed to *participate* in it, not just *attend* it."

This time Helene did roll her eyes. "I don't understand what this"—she waved her hands around the room—"is going to solve. You think I chased Sara out of town and that I'm being overbearing with Tasha." Helene pointed at Dr. Austen. "She can't fix what you think."

Dr. Austen jotted down something in her notebook.

"What did you just write down?" Helene leaned forward. "Say something. I know how much we're paying for this session when we could use the money to rent that beautiful pergola for Tasha's wedding ceremony."

"Tasha doesn't want it." Max rubbed his forehead before looking at Dr. Austen. "See? She doesn't listen. It wasn't always like this, but it has gotten to the point where she doesn't hear a word anyone says. Half the time, I don't think she even listens to herself."

"That's not true," said Helene as she carefully folded her hands in her lap. She had no desire for Dr. Austen to interpret her fidgeting as a nervous tick or expression of guilt or shame. Her feelings were her own business and no one else's. "The problem is no one has anything helpful to say."

Max stood up and shook his head. "You see?" he asked Dr. Austen. "I told her before we came today that unless she's willing to give therapy one-hundred-percent effort on her part, I'm done. I will not spend any more time watching her alienate herself from her family and friends. Our daughter is getting remarried in ten weeks. Helene has until the wedding to figure out why she keeps pushing everyone away."

"I don't push people away, Max. You're exaggerating."

He put his hands on the side of the chair and looked at her. Helene stared back at him and blinked several times at what she saw.

The man in front of her looked like her husband, but instead of a happy smile, his mouth scowled back at her. Where his eyes used to twinkle when he gazed at her, Max's dull stare made her shiver. The clothes he wore seemed too big. Had he lost weight?

"Are you okay? You don't look well."

Throwing his hands in the air, Max turned to Dr. Austen. "You see this, right? She is so wrapped up in whatever is going on inside her head that she has no clue what her behavior is doing to other people." Dropping back down in the chair, Max continued, "I've spent so much time trying to repair the damage

Helene has done that I'm resentful of it. I don't look well because I'm exhausted. All I do these days is apologize for her and her behavior. I've had enough.

"We've got ten weeks to figure this out. If Helene can't come up with some way to pull her head out of her ass, then I'm done."

"Maxwell, watch your language," Helene said as she grabbed for his hand. Max pulled it away, and Helene's stomach clenched. He was serious. A quick glance at Dr. Austen revealed the therapist was scrutinizing her. "Fine. I'll talk with Dr. Austen for the next ten weeks."

"You won't just talk to her. You'll make some changes." Max stood up again and walked toward the door. "This is your last chance, Helene. I love you, but I don't love who you've become. I want back the girl I married. We weren't perfect then, but at least I could support the things you stood for. Lately, your behavior makes me question if the old you is still in there."

He nodded to Dr. Austen before leaving the room.

Helene closed her eyes and took a deep breath. She couldn't believe the situation in which she found herself. This wasn't the way her marriage was supposed to end. Although it was a fitting close to the way it had started.

She opened her eyes at the sound of Dr. Austen clearing her throat.

Pen poised over the pad of paper in her lap, the doctor said, "Well, it looks like we have our work cut out for us."

2

"I suppose this is where you ask me about my childhood, right?" Helene twisted her wedding ring. The one-and-a-half-carat princess-cut diamond comforted her despite the situation. "I've heard everything stems from that. My daughters would agree with you—Sara particularly. It's all my fault she moved to Chicago. At least now that Tasha is engaged to Greg she seems to be easier to be around."

Dr. Austen shrugged. "We can start wherever you're comfortable." She glanced down at her notes. "I will say that with only ten weeks to come to a resolution, we are under a bit of a time crunch."

Helene waved her hand. "As long as I'm working on it, Max will give us an extension."

Instead of the automatic agreement she expected, Helene paused as Dr. Austen frowned.

"I don't think you understand the seriousness of this. Your husband has been seeing me for several months, ever since you outed"—she glanced down at her notes as if confirming details—"Brad Gerome and his boyfriend, Carlton. And from the list of things you've interfered with, I have to agree that something needs to change."

Helene popped up from the chair.

"I did no such thing. Brad's relationship was obvious to everyone. This has nothing to do with why I'm here, anyway. Brad and Carlton are happy. They're having a baby. Don't tell me Brad's complaining about me as well?"

Crossing her legs, Dr. Austen steepled her fingers together and rested her chin on her forefingers as Helene continued ranting.

"I bet next you're going to tell me I should never have sent Tasha to speed dating. Well, if I hadn't intervened, she never would have met Greg and they wouldn't be getting married."

Dr. Austen raised a hand. "She already knew Greg. I believe he's your grandson's soccer coach."

Eyebrows furrowed, Helene ignored the interruption and barrelled on.

"And don't get me started on Sara. My eldest daughter would never have had to move to Chicago if she'd just accepted my gift of the relationship coordinator. What a waste of money. That receptionist at her old law firm is going to get the man of her dreams, and Sara will be left to waste away."

"But didn't *you* want to move to Chicago?"

The question stopped Helene. Max had been thorough when he gave their life history to this woman. Indignation disguised as heartburn flared in her chest.

"Of course I did. I wanted to be anywhere other than Glen Valley. There is nothing good about that town."

"Tell me where you grew up."

Helene shook her head. "What did I tell you? Typical for the therapist to blame the childhood for what I am today."

Dr. Austen shrugged. "Indulge me. Tell me about growing up. I understand you were an only child raised by your grandparents. Do you remember your parents at all?"

Helene turned away from Dr. Austen. If she was ever going to get home and work on the wedding arrangements for Tasha, she needed to put this therapy session in high gear. Clearly, two could play at this game. Helene turned back to face Dr. Austen.

"It was my sixth birthday," Helene said. She wondered what Max would say when he found out she'd told the marriage therapist about the party memory. He was the only person alive she'd trusted with it, and look where that got her: a therapist's office. "Mommy made a chocolate birthday cake for me and my friends.

"We were all outside. Someone tacked a pin-the-tail-on-the-donkey game on the shed, and we had hula hoops, and I remember the clown." She smiled. "Edith, one of the girls from the neighborhood, had to go home because the clown scared her. But not me. I thought he was great."

Helene leaned back into her seat as she remembered that day.

CLARENCE THE CLOWN sported bright-red curly hair that matched his bulbous plastic nose and big, floppy red shoes. Helene loved the scratchy feel of Clarence's rainbow-striped jacket and pants. For some reason, she couldn't stop grabbing his leg.

"Leave the clown alone, Helene," her dad had said, then took a swig from the glass in his hand. "You're not a baby anymore."

"She's fine, Glenn. Leave her be," her mother said. She stood by the cake table, sipping her wine. She smiled at Helene before inhaling deeply from her cigarette. Helene grinned at the rings of smoke that passed out of her mother's mouth. "It's her birthday. If she wants to hug the clown, she can."

Her father emptied his glass and headed to the makeshift bar.

"She's never gonna grow up if you don't teach her some manners. But fine. If that's the way you want it, then she's your problem."

Helene watched her father walk away before turning back to her mom.

"It's okay, sweetie. Daddy's in a bad mood. It's your birthday. Do whatever you want."

For the rest of the party, Helene stayed within reach of the clown. She didn't know why she liked him so much. Maybe it was because her father didn't like him. Even at six years old, she didn't feel the same way about her father as she did her mommy. He wasn't like Edith's daddy, who hugged and kissed her as soon as he got home from work. Helene's daddy went straight to the bar, and he yelled at her if she appeared before he'd finished his first drink.

When it was time to blow out the candles, Daddy picked her up and held her over the cake.

"Hurry up and make a wish. The guys are meeting at the bar," her father said. She felt her father sway forward, and the cake was close enough she could put her finger in the frosting.

Someone called out, "Don't fall in the cake, Glenn. You'll never live that one down."

Her daddy cleared his throat when he steadied himself, then took a swig from his glass. Helene slipped a little from her perch and struggled to remain in her father's arms. He glanced down at her.

"You're heavy." Without warning, he set her on the ground. "Blow out the candles from there."

She wanted to complain, but Helene knew better. Daddy hated it when anyone talked back to him. Mommy had stayed inside for a whole week once when Daddy smacked her for lipping off. The memory of her mother's black eye gave Helene an idea.

Closing her eyes, Helene blew out the candles and made her birthday wish.

"That was the night your parents died?"

Helene jerked at the sound of Dr. Austen's voice. That was the closest she'd ever come to revealing what she'd wished for that night. She brushed away the tear that rolled down her cheek and leaned down for her purse. A movement caught her eye, and she glanced up. Dr. Austen's eyes caught hold of hers as she held out a box of tissues.

Unease swept over Helene as the therapist examined her face, but Helene reassured herself.

She has no idea what I wished for that night. She can't read my mind. I'm the only one who knows.

Helene pulled out several tissues and dabbed her cheeks. She needed to find her powder to repair the damage the tears had done to her foundation, but tissue would suffice for now.

Rather than thanking the therapist for her gesture, Helene answered the question. "Yes. That's correct."

"And you know what happened?"

"My parents' car hit a tree. They died on impact." She swallowed hard. Despite the knowledge that her wish hadn't actually caused it, her parents' accident always hit a nerve. She never talked about their demise, and she didn't plan to start now. She planned on taking her secret to her grave. "No witnesses. No way of knowing exactly what happened."

Dr. Austen looked down at her notes. "Max seems to think the reason you've become . . . ," Dr. Austen paused as if searching for the right word, "overbearing, if you will, is because of what happened to your parents." She placed the paper in her notebook, closed it, and sat back.

Helene clenched her teeth. The audacity of this woman, thinking she understood anything about her. How dare she make judgments about how her life had ended up this way? There was nothing Helene could have done about her parents. She was only a child and hadn't understood the situation. Grammy bore the guilt of not doing anything, and that was just fine with Helene.

"Do you think that's an accurate statement?"

Tensing at the question, Helene reached into her purse and pulled out her mirrored compact. She reapplied her powder as she made Dr. Austen wait on her response.

Oh, how she hated that word. *Overbearing* sounded so negative. All she ever did was to make sure her family didn't make preventable mistakes. She, of all people, knew what happened when someone made a wish that couldn't be reversed, and she had lived with the consequences. Helene promised herself she would never let down anyone in her family. She would fight for them the way no one had fought for her.

Helene checked her handiwork in her mirror. Satisfied with the results, she clicked the compact shut and returned her gaze to the therapist. Dr. Austen wore a grim smile.

Good. Now you know who's in control.

"No, I do not think I'm overbearing, if that's what you mean. My intent is pure. I want what is best for my family and I'll do whatever it takes to make that happen."

Helene settled back in her chair and crossed her legs. There was nothing wrong with her life. She might not be living in her dream location, but she'd long ago made peace with the fact that Glen Valley would have to do. She'd made it work. She'd raised two children here. Supported her husband. Made a name for herself. Just because not everyone liked the way she did things didn't mean it was her problem.

She had learned long ago that she couldn't control what other people thought about her. But she could control herself.

And she would, regardless of whatever this smug therapist threw at her.

3

Max adjusted the napkin and stepped back from the dinner table. The silver was polished, the china set, and the crystal sparkled. He wanted everything to be perfect for Helene when she got home. Their first appointment with the marriage counselor hadn't gone as planned. It hadn't helped matters that he'd lost his temper and left the office.

Running his hands through his thinning gray hair, he questioned whether he had done the right thing. He loved his wife. He wouldn't have put up with thirty-seven years of marriage if he didn't. He understood she'd experienced things he couldn't imagine, and he gave her leeway because of it.

But had he let her go too far? Should he have stopped this nonsense years ago? Was it too late?

The ringing of the telephone interrupted his thoughts, and he walked into the kitchen in search of his cell phone. He smiled when he saw Tasha's number on caller ID.

"Hi, honey. How are you?" Max asked.

"Good. I just wanted to see how the therapy session went. And if you need any help with dinner."

"The session was fine, and I've got dinner in the oven. All I have to do is follow the reheating instructions." He didn't want to bother their daughter any more than he had to. "What could go wrong?"

Tasha laughed. "Based on that question, I'm guessing Mom was pissed off after talking with a therapist. Which is why you're treating her to all her favorite foods? Do you have the eggplant Parmesan in the oven? It needs at least an hour to cook. The Caesar salad's in the fridge with the garlic bread and the tiramisu."

"Did I tell you about the bakery down the street from Sara's office that makes the world's greatest tiramisu?" Max asked. "Too bad I didn't think of this sooner. She could have shipped it to me."

Tasha cleared her throat. "If she knew it was for Mom, I'm not sure she would help. She's still upset over how things were left."

His smile vanished. "Well, thank you for helping me plan this. I know your mother is a bit over-the-top lately—"

"When is she not?" asked Tasha. "Although, therapy might distract her from my wedding. Greg's being so nice about things, but he has no interest in being carried down the aisle by his groomsmen on a litter. Where did she even come up with that?"

"We watched *Cleopatra* a few weeks ago," said Max. "I thought it would take her mind off the wedding and give you kids a break. Seems like it backfired."

He relaxed at the sound of his daughter's laughter.

"You are the best dad ever, you know that?" said Tasha.

The alarm on the microwave went off, signaling the eggplant Parm was ready.

"Gotta go. That's the timer."

"Okay. I love you. Good luck tonight," said Tasha.

Hoping he wouldn't need luck, Max grabbed the hot pads

from the counter and flung open the stove door. Steam from the golden-brown cheese hit his face, and he removed the dish from the oven, gently placing it on the trivet. It needed to rest for a few minutes, but Helene should be home anytime.

"Wine. That's what I forgot. She'll want a glass of wine when she gets home."

Kicking himself for not making a list of things he should do to prepare for dinner, Max hurried to the fridge. He removed a chilled bottle of Helene's favored rosé before rummaging around in the kitchen drawer in search of the corkscrew.

"It has to be here somewhere," he muttered to himself. Finding the corkscrew lodged behind the lemon juicer thingy, he went to work opening the bottle. After a brief struggle, the cork popped off. Shaking his head, he said, "They really should make these screw tops," as he replaced the corkscrew.

He took the bottle to the dining room and poured wine into each of the glasses he had set on the table. Knowing what they had both been through with Dr. Austen that afternoon, he wanted to be sure to make tonight as pleasant as possible.

As he stepped back from the table, he recalled all the efforts Helene had made for him during their marriage. He leaned against the wall as he considered the functions, happy hours, and dinner parties she'd coordinated and cooked for. He was a basket case with this meal, and he'd done nothing more than heat it up. Maybe he should give his wife some slack.

His generosity gave way to irritation then worry as he sat at the dinner table three hours later, sipping wine alone. He had suspected Helene would be annoyed with the therapist, but he hadn't thought she wouldn't come home after the appointment. He checked his cell phone for the umpteenth time. No text. No phone call. No message.

Debating whether to leave another message, he decided the one he'd left an hour ago was enough.

Your appointment ended a while ago. I know you didn't want to go, but I'm worried. Please call me back.

He headed back to the kitchen to check on the eggplant Parmesan. He'd put it back in the oven to keep it warm, but he was worried it would dry out. Helene wouldn't eat Parmesan unless it was perfect, that he knew. He predicted she would blame the dried-out casserole on him rather than accept the fact that she was the one late for dinner.

"Damn it." He slammed his hand onto the counter. "This is exactly why we need Dr. Austen."

Marriage was a give-and-take institution. He knew that. Helene had given up a lot to support him through the years. He knew, as well as everyone else in the tri-state area, that she hadn't wanted to live in his hometown. But that didn't give her an excuse to complain all the time and manipulate people and make him worry about her.

When he heard the sound of the garage door opening, he didn't know whether to be relieved or furious. He refilled the glasses of wine to keep himself busy as he waited for his wife to come inside.

"Max, can you help me, please?"

His head sagged as he let out a sigh. She didn't even acknowledge the fact that she was late. As usual, it was all about her.

Wine sloshed out of the glass as he hastily set it down and made his way to the garage. He stopped short when he saw her holding bags from the bridal shop.

"You went shopping?"

"Of course. There are only ten weeks to Tasha's wedding, as you pointed out to Dr. Austen. I'll attend those silly appointments, but I have to keep working on my part of the wedding." She held out several bags for him. "Well, don't just stand there. Help me take these inside."

He shuffled over to her and grabbed three bags.

"Max! Be careful! Those bags have crowns in them. They're fragile."

Peeking inside the first bag, he asked, "Why does Tasha need a crown?"

Helene threw her arms in the air. "You never listen to me. I read you the article from the bridal magazine. Crowns are the 'it' accessory of the season. You can't get married without one."

Grateful for the glass of wine he left on the counter, Max took the bags his wife handed him and walked back inside. He gently placed the bags on the kitchen table, then sipped wine as he waited for Helene to follow him.

He waited another five minutes before she came in, a small cooler with wheels trailing behind her. Frowning, he pointed with his glass.

"What's that?"

"Cake samples."

Nodding, he watched as she transferred small white boxes with pink and black labels from the cooler to the fridge.

"And what are you doing with cake samples? The last I recall, Tasha said she didn't want a cake. She planned to serve gluten-free, vegan donuts at the reception."

Helene turned from what she was doing to look at him. With her hands on her hips, he expected a lecture on the uncouthness of donuts, but instead she asked, "What is that smell?"

Max put down his glass and hurried over to the oven. He opened the door and, with a flourish of his hand, said, "Dinner. Eggplant Parmesan. Your favorite. I thought I would do something nice for you after your first therapy session." He crossed his arms over his chest. He kept his voice calm when he added, "But it was ready hours ago because you neglected to inform me of your shopping extravaganza. Does that seem strange to you?"

At first, he thought she caught the sarcasm in his voice, but he was disappointed when she said, "Why would it be strange? You know I have a lot to do with the wedding. And we talked about the fact that I need to lose five more pounds to look good in my mother-of-the-bride dress. I'll just have salad tonight."

Max narrowed his eyes as Helene continued unloading the cooler. The audacity of her behavior, particularly after the conversation they'd had with Dr. Austen today, made him wonder once again: was he wasting his time?

"Well, I have to eat, so I'm going to sit down at the table and enjoy this. The Parm is—well, *was*—fresh, and there's Caesar salad and garlic bread and tiramisu for dessert." He gestured to the glass of rosé on the counter, even though Helene was paying more attention to the cake than she was to him. "Here's a glass of wine if you want it. If not, I'll drink it."

Without looking up, Helene said, "You shouldn't have too much alcohol. It'll give you heartburn." She continued unloading boxes and said, "I don't want you waking me up tonight. I have an early appointment with another string ensemble. I just didn't get a good feel for the viola player. Too much of a renegade if you ask me. She wanted to play that song about a thousand years. Can you imagine that?"

He didn't have the energy to bother asking what the problem was with the song, so he pulled the casserole from the oven and scooped out a big piece. He took it and his wine to the living room and settled into his recliner. If his wife wasn't going to pay attention to him, he sure as hell wasn't going to listen to her complain about a wedding that no one had asked her to coordinate.

4

"Now, this box contains a slice of chocolate fudge cake with a coconut-caramel filling and chocolate-coconut buttercream icing," said Helene as she pushed the box in front of Tasha. "It would be perfect for Greg's groom's cake."

She looked down at her checklist. Her daughter had vetoed eight of the twenty samples she'd offered so far. If this kept up, Helene would need to find more options. She didn't understand why Tasha was being so picky. Helene was doing the heavy lifting when it came to the wedding. She expected Tasha to show some gratitude.

"Mom, I told you Greg is allergic to coconut, which is why, every time you give me a sample of cake that has coconut in it, I say no."

Helene frowned. "But *you're* not allergic. Why can't you have something *you* like?"

Tasha closed her eyes, and Helene swore she saw her daughter's lips counting to ten.

"What are you doing?" Helene checked her watch. "We still need to get through the rest of the cakes, and then I want you to try on the crowns I brought. If we pick a crown, it might inspire the look of the dress."

Pushing back from the kitchen island, Tasha shook her head. "Mother, I've got this covered. It's my second wedding, and Greg and I agreed we don't want anything big. We'd rather elope than do this."

Helene frowned. "You can't do that. I already put down a deposit at the Wedding Stable. We need to make this the wedding of the century. Your first one with Doug was terrible. I can't believe you got married in the courthouse. Even *I* got married in a church." Helene paused as she thought about the day she had stood alone in the bridal suite, wondering if she should go through with the wedding or not. Shaking her head, she knew now wasn't the time to go down memory lane. She continued, "Besides, I want Doug's mother to be so jealous she wasn't invited that she'll beg me to join her committee at the country club."

She checked her list to see what cake sample was next.

"Here's something without coconut. It's a white cake with raspberry flavoring, lemon curd filling, and a white chocolate ganache." She slid the box over to where Tasha sat. "I suppose you could make it a drip cake if you wanted. They are so 2015, but if it's what you want, I'd be fine with it."

When Tasha didn't touch the cake or make a response, Helene looked up to see that her daughter was standing on the other side of the kitchen, gathering up her purse.

"Where do you think you're going? We have a lot of work to do."

Tasha slid the crossbody strap of her handbag over her head and nodded. "Yes. We do. *I* need to plan *my* wedding. *You* need to work on *your* marriage." She leaned back on the counter. "Dad is serious about the therapy."

Helene's cheeks flushed. "How do you know about that?"

"Who do you think recommended eggplant Parmesan? Or

the tiramisu? Neither of which you ate, by the way. Dad told me you think you need to lose weight, which is ridiculous. You look great." Helene recognized the feisty look on her daughter's face as Tasha struck a model pose and winked. "No one is going to be looking at you during the wedding anyway. They're going to be looking at me."

"All the more reason to pick a breathtaking gown and crown! You know that is somewhat self-centered of you to say."

"Self-centered of *me*? Listen to yourself. This is my wedding, which I do not want your help with, nor did I ever ask for your help." A serious expression replaced Tasha's feisty one. "Mom, you have to rein it in. Sara won't commit to being maid of honor because she doesn't want to be around when you take over. And all Dad wants is for the two of you to be like you used to be—before you got all controlling and became that lady in *The Devil Wears Prada*. If you don't take this marriage therapy seriously, you're going to be the one alone. I can take care of myself. You need to do the same." Tasha glanced at the rest of the cakes. "I'll take the rest of the samples home for the twins. Blake was upset that he couldn't come over, and I promised him a few tastes."

Frustrated with her daughter, Helene shrugged her shoulders. "At least let me know what ones you liked the best. If you insist on doing something uncouth like donuts, maybe you should consider cupcakes. The baker can do any of these flavors in regular or mini-sized cupcakes and arrange them in a tower for the wedding. I thought you might like that."

She almost lost her balance when Tasha grabbed her shoulders and pulled her in for a hug.

"That is a great idea! Thank you. I still like the donut idea, but cupcakes make a great backup plan."

When Tasha let her go, Helene relished the look of genuine happiness on her daughter's face. She didn't get a bright smile like that often.

Maybe the therapist is right, she thought. *Perhaps I should back off a bit.*

Testing her luck, Helene asked, "What about the crowns? You could take those home too and let Libby help you pick one."

Tasha shook her head. "You don't know how to stop when you're ahead. I don't want a crown, and I'm not letting you use Libby to manipulate me."

Knowing she could drop by the house later in the week and show the crowns to her granddaughter, Helene helped Tasha load up the cakes and carry them to the car. She walked back into the kitchen after seeing her daughter off and reluctantly dug out a piece of paper from her purse: her assignment from Dr. Austen.

Helene studied the list of situations the therapist had asked her to write down. Supposedly, if she wrote out her feelings about all these scenarios, she might get some insight into whether her current situation resulted from her childhood.

The list was long, and the task was ridiculous as far as Helene was concerned. Pushing it aside, Helene looked around the kitchen. She had more pressing things to do than write about her childhood. Like cleaning the oven.

Helene clicked her tongue at the sight of her oven. When Max had heated up that Parmesan, some of it had spilled over and burnt to the bottom. While she planned to have a word with Max about his mess, cleaning the oven sounded like a better use of her time than rehashing long-ago events of her life.

Helene donned her apron, making sure the blouse underneath was completely covered. She grabbed her thick rubber gloves from under the sink, as well as the oven cleaner, and went to work.

As she scraped off all the loose bits of charred food, Helene remembered how Grammy insisted elbow grease was the only proper way to clean an oven. She continued her task as memories of cleaning her grandmother's oven filled her mind.

"BUT WHY CAN'T I just use the oven cleaner, Grammy? The foamy stuff melts down the gunk on the sides and it just wipes off. Mommy used it."

As soon as she mentioned her mother, Helene tensed. Grammy got mad when she talked about her mommy and made her do more chores. Pressing her lips together, Helene hoped Grammy hadn't heard her.

"Because you live in my house and you will do as I say. Now, keep scrubbing. After the oven, you've got the floor to mop. And this week, you best do it well. Don't think I don't know how you swept all the crumbs to the corners. My back ached cleaning up after you."

Rather than argue with her grandmother, Helene shoved her head back into the oven and scrubbed. She'd never cleaned this much when her mommy and daddy were alive. But ever since she'd moved in with Grammy and Pappy, all she did was clean. The kids at her new school called her Cinderella. She hated the nickname. Grammy told her not to talk with any of the other children, that they would be mean to her. Helene knew Grammy was right, but all she wanted was a friend.

When she'd shown up at school with black soot stains on her shirt from the fireplace, one of her classmates made fun of her.

"She's all dirty," teased the girl. "Don't you have clean clothes?"

Helene blushed as she looked down at her shirt. "I had to clean the fireplace for my grandmother. Her back hurts so she can't do it herself."

"So, you're like Cinderella, only instead of an evil stepmother, you have an evil grandmother."

"She's not evil," said Helene. "She just needs my help."

No one listened to her, though. The kids continued to call her Cinderella, and she played by herself at recess, never making any friends at that school.

Nor had she made any at the next one or the next one. It wasn't until she made it to high school that she found anyone she could relate to. And it looked like she was going to lose that friend too if she didn't do what this quack of a marriage therapist wanted.

She peeled off her gloves and apron and flung them into the kitchen sink before rummaging around in a kitchen drawer, looking for a notebook and a pen. If this assignment was going to distract her from cleaning the oven, she might as well do it now.

It certainly wasn't because she thought Max was serious about this ten-week ultimatum.

5

Dropping the notebook and pen onto the kitchen table, Helene poured herself a glass of wine before sitting down to write.

"It's five o'clock somewhere," she muttered as she stared down at the sheet Dr. Austen had given her.

"Write about something in your childhood that made you uncomfortable. It could be a situation at home, at school, or in an extracurricular activity."

"What didn't make me feel uncomfortable in those days?" Helene muttered to herself. Swirling the wine in her glass, she considered her options. What could she tell this therapist to get her off her back? She'd talked about her parents during her first session, so she didn't see the need to revisit that. There had to be something else that would satisfy the doctor.

The constant moving as a child might make for a good journal entry. Technically, the reason for all the moves was for her grandfather's job. He'd had some sort of government position that required them to relocate every few years. At least, that's what she remembered.

Come to think of it, all the moves had coincided with some

sort of incident at school. It never failed that, shortly after Grammy got a call from a principal, counselor, or teacher, Pappy announced they were moving.

Helene put down her wine glass. She jotted down a list of all the schools she'd attended along with the dates she'd been there. Then she made a note of incidents that had happened.

It didn't take long to prove the pattern. At the school where she was called Cinderella, the counselor had called Grammy, complaining that Helene's chores were too dangerous for her age. The next week, they had moved.

Helene cringed as she recalled the incident where the teacher had told Grammy she was too old to parent Helene. Grammy's words could be heard out in the hall where Helene had been told to wait during the parent-teacher conference.

"I'm not her momma. I'm her grandmomma. And I'm well aware of my age. There ain't anything I can do about that, but there is something you can do about your disrespect. In fact, I'll do somethin' about it too." Grammy had reported the teacher to the principal, but Helene never made it back to that classroom.

One school didn't fit the pattern, though. Helene dropped her pen and sipped her wine as she recalled the lunchroom incident with Dorothy and the principal who'd protected her.

Looking around the lunchroom, Helene spotted an empty table in the corner of the room. She made a beeline for it. She didn't want anyone near her when she took out her liver and onion sandwich. It smelled almost as disgusting as it tasted.

Helene hunched over her brown paper bag and carefully pulled out her sandwich. She rolled the bag back up and tucked it next to her on the bench. Experience taught her it was safer to eat one thing at a time. That way, if someone threw her lunch on the ground, she only lost one part of it. She would still have a piece of fruit or jerky left over that would keep her stomach from rumbling during the afternoon. She'd learned her lesson earlier that year. After her teacher had called her grandmother, Grammy hadn't fed her dinner for a week.

"That's what it's like to be hungry. Now, don't go whinin' to that teacher of yours. It makes things worse, ya see."

She'd made it halfway through the sandwich before Dorothy and her gaggle of followers entered the cafeteria. It made Helene happy to call the girl Dorothy in her head. The bully preferred Dot, but what she didn't know wouldn't hurt her.

The girls stopped in a huddle and looked around the room. Helene followed their gaze as it settled on the table where she sat. The sandwich Helene had swallowed threatened to come back up.

Knowing what came next, Helene stuffed her sandwich into her lunch sack and prepared to be ejected from the table. She preferred to retreat rather than listen to all the vile things the girls said. They were mean to everyone. Herself included.

As she left the table, Helene heard Dorothy.

"I told you all we had to do was head this way and that smelly hag would leave. She's too stupid to stand up for herself."

Helene walked toward the exit, discreetly sniffing her shirt. She only got one bath a week, but she usually didn't smell until Friday. Wondering if she could convince Grammy to let her bathe midweek, Helene was almost to the door when Dorothy called out, "I should teach you some manners."

Helene's feet froze. Daddy had threatened her like that and then he died after her birthday wish. As much as she wanted to punish Dorothy for being a bully, she didn't want her dead. Forcing her feet to move, Helene headed to the safety of the exit. As she pushed the door open, Dorothy laughed.

"I told you. She's a big loser."

Helene slowly turned and looked back at the table she'd escaped. The girls talked and laughed as they spread out their lunches, going on with their day as if nothing had happened. No one paid attention to Helene as she watched. No one in the room cared that she was upset. Her shoulders sagged.

She doubted anyone in this town cared she was alive. Maybe Pappy. He always made time for her. Grammy didn't. Her grandmother made it clear she was a bother above all else.

"If I didn't have to raise you, I'd be a happy woman."

Helene licked her lips nervously. Maybe this was her chance to prove herself. If she stood up for herself, Grammy might be pleased with her.

Gathering all her nerve, Helene shuffled back to the table, stood behind Dorothy, and waited. When the girl on the opposite side of the table pointed at her, Helene tensed. No changing her mind now.

Dorothy turned and frowned. "What are you looking at, loser?"

For once, Helene stared back at Dorothy. The girl blinked. If they'd been in a staring competition, Helene would have won. But this wasn't a game. Not this time.

"I said, what are you staring at? Or don't you know how to speak?" Dorothy elbowed the girl next to her. "My mom said abandoned children aren't very bright. That explains a lot about her."

Before she knew what was happening, Helene said, "I'm not abandoned. And I'm not stupid."

Dorothy's table fell silent as Helene felt six pairs of eyes bore into her.

"Well, who would've guessed?" Dorothy asked as she stood up from the table and towered over Helene. "The runt speaks."

The lunch bag shook, and she hid it behind her back. Whatever she planned to say to Dorothy had vanished, and Helene stood there, dumbfounded.

"What else do ya have to say?" The bully stepped closer, so close Helene smelled the tuna fish on Dorothy's breath. She envied the girl. Tuna fish smelled better than liver and onions. Her attention jerked back to Dorothy's eyes when the girl said, "I asked you a question."

Before Helene could respond, someone shoved her from behind, and she fell into Dorothy. Her forehead slammed into the girl's sternum and bounced off. The unexpected motion sent her falling to the cold cafeteria floor.

She glanced up in time to see Dorothy flail, grabbing for anything to regain her balance. Dorothy held onto the table to steady herself, but it wasn't enough, and she fell into the girl next to her. A tray of food flipped over, spilling its contents on Dorothy's back.

Mashed potatoes and gravy dripped off Dorothy's shoulder, and Helene's stomach rumbled.

She didn't know for sure if the pain in her stomach was hunger or worry. She never should have come back to the table. Dorothy was a bully, just like Daddy was. As she pulled herself off the floor, she heard Dorothy's ultimatum.

"Park. After school. Just you and me. We're going to end this once and for all."

Helene blinked up at Dorothy. If she got caught fighting, Grammy would be furious. One of the teachers from school would be sure to call her grandmother, and Helene would never hear the end of it.

But if she didn't stand up for herself now, Dorothy would keep bullying her.

As she opened her mouth to answer, the laughter and taunting stopped. Helene noticed everyone looking over her shoulder. Something told her whatever was behind her was worse than what was in front of her.

Helene slowly turned around. The principal stood there,

her arms crossed, taking in the situation. Helene's stomach churned at the expression on the principal's face.

"Dorothy, we've discussed this before. Fighting is not a way to resolve a situation." The principal glanced down at Helene, nodded, then looked back at Dorothy and her gang. "This entire table is to report to my office." When no one moved, she said, "Now."

Helene remained where she stood until the rest of the girls were a few feet away before she followed.

"Helene. Wait."

She halted in surprise. She'd never seen the principal at this school yell at students in front of other children. Helene was used to getting in trouble, but she didn't like being publicly chastised.

"Are you okay?" the principal asked Helene. "Your forehead is red. Did someone hit you?"

"No, ma'am." Helene knew from experience that the less she said, the safer she would be. From Dorothy and from Grammy. "My head hit Dorothy." Helene caught herself. "I mean Dot."

A brief smile crossed the woman's face. Relieved that she didn't have to explain herself, Helene hugged her lunch bag closer. The gesture drew the principal's gaze. "Liver and onions again?"

She lowered her eyes to the floor and nodded. Helene felt the principal's hand push her gently toward the back of the room.

"Come on. Let's get you something good to eat before I go deal with Dorothy. But you have to promise not to tell your grandmother. The last time you got cafeteria food, she complained to me. Said she'd pull you out of school if you ate for free again. But I can't have that. I need good students like you."

. . .

Helene exhaled slowly, stunned at all the notes she'd written. She reached for her wine to find an empty glass. Pushing away from the table, she got up for a refill and to mull over what she'd discovered.

That incident should have triggered a move, but she'd stayed there for the rest of the school year. Come to think of it, she'd been there two more years. And Dorothy never bothered her again.

After she poured more wine, she gazed out the kitchen window. Oh, how she loved this backyard. Max had searched high and low for a house with some place his family could play and make memories. A swing set stood in one corner. Not the one from Sara and Tasha's childhood but a new one that was safe for Libby and Blake. Her husband had gone out of his way to make things nice for her and their children and grandchildren.

The thought of her grandchildren made her smile. What would Libby look like wearing one of the crowns she'd picked up for Tasha? If she hadn't had a glass of wine, she'd head over there now, but now it would have to wait until tomorrow. At least she had the house to herself. Max was busy with his Thursday night bowling league.

Helene could finish her glass of wine while going through the notes she'd made for Tasha's wedding. If she couldn't convince Greg to be carried into the ceremony on a litter by his groomsmen, maybe he'd be amenable to a dog as a ring bearer.

6

The slamming of the bowling ball into the pins made it hard to hear the announcements.

"Holy Rollers versus Bad Boy Ballers on lane three, not lane five! Can't you hear me, Ballers?"

Claude placed his rainbow-colored bowling ball on the return and sat down. "How come they get a cool name like that and we have to be the Geezer Glens?"

"Why do you ask the same question every week?" Pete asked back.

Max blew out a breath. As glad as he was for the distraction from Helene and therapy, he didn't know if he had the strength to listen to Claude and Pete bicker like an old married couple tonight. Sure, it was funny for a while, but Max knew the routine. The men started with the names of the other bowling teams, then they moved to the city council budget, and they always ended with a rousing argument of which Baptist church in town was better. Considering there were only two, it was a fifty-fifty shot.

Frank nudged his ribcage. "Gets old, don't it?"

Max nodded, knowing that if he engaged in small talk with

Frank this early in the evening, he'd want to leave before they started the second game of the match. A little of Frank went a long way. Kind of like Helene these days.

He shook his head. He had to stop thinking like that. Marriage therapy was going to work. Helene was working on her assignment from Dr. Austen. She'd told him about the food fight when she was in junior high school.

"Food fight" wasn't exactly the right description, but it did make him understand how hard it had been on her growing up with her grandparents. They hadn't been equipped to raise a grandchild. Not after what happened to Helene's mother. Not that he was supposed to know about that.

Frank nudged him again. "You seem distracted tonight. Everything okay?"

Sharing his troubles with Frank was a surefire way for everyone in the league to know his business. He'd done it once before, after Tasha had ended things with her ex-husband while he was in the hospital. Only problem was, Frank got the story wrong. For the next two weeks, Max had fielded questions about how Tasha put Doug in the hospital. He never wanted to experience that again.

"Focusing on my game, that's all." He pulled his bowling ball from its bag and gently placed it on the return. Giving it a little pat, he said, "You best focus too. If we don't cream the Incredibowls, we'll never hear the end of it. Remember last year?"

Frank took the bait and rattled on about the unfairness of the previous year's semifinals while Max laced up his bowling shoes. Pleased with his work, Max leaned back in the hard plastic seats and listened to his teammate complain.

By the eighth frame, Max discovered his distraction had worked a little too well. Frank regaled them all with a detailed breakdown of their mistakes over and over again.

"It's been a year, Frank," Claude said as he wiped his lucky fifteen-pounder dry. "I got my hernia fixed so I won't drop the ball on anyone's foot again. I promise."

Before anymore smack talk started, Max waved at the guys. "I'm heading to the bar. Anyone want anything?"

"Does a fish need water to live?" asked Pete. "Of course, I need another beer. Get a round for all of us."

Claude shook his head and patted his stomach. "Diet soda. Maurine's got me on a diet."

"Do they have a light beer?" Frank called out from the lane. "I've been bloated lately after drinking the regular stuff."

Turning away before the guys could see him roll his eyes, Max strolled to the bar. Man, his teammates were getting old. He scanned the bowling alley, waving at a friend here and there. Frowning, he realized it wasn't just his teammates getting old. Everyone in this bowling alley looked north of sixty. Hell, they were all senior citizens.

Max approached the bar and got in line. He scanned the menu board, despite knowing exactly what was served, when he heard the man in front of him speak.

"Hear you're getting ready for another wedding," said Roger Gerome. "Hope this one turns out better than Tasha's first."

Damn. Why wasn't I paying attention to who was in front of me?

It was bad enough his daughter's ex-father-in-law played in the same bowling league, but to make matters worse, he was the captain of last year's champions, E-Bowla. Stupid team name in Max's opinion, but stupid or not, the team had talent.

Max accepted Roger's extended hand to shake, wishing he didn't have to be polite. He'd known Roger since kindergarten, long before Tasha married Roger's douche bag of a son. Max didn't like today's Roger any more than the five-year-old version who ate his own boogers during nap time.

"We're all excited for Tasha. Greg's a great guy," said Max, subtly wiping his hand on his pants. Not wanting to engage in a lengthy conversation, Max asked, "How's Doug?"

"Great. Started a new business. Seeing a hot chick," Roger said, nudging Max with an elbow. "You know my boy. Has an eye for the women."

Max started to mention that Doug's eye for women was what had ended his daughter's marriage, but the teenager behind the counter spoke first.

"Here's your order, Mr. Gerome," she said as she pushed a tray of food toward him.

"No charge, of course." Roger winked at the girl, then turned to Max. "Perk of being a league champion. Free food for a year."

Max nodded and watched the man walk away. Roger was and always would be an asshole. Not for the first time did Max wonder how Roger's other son Brad had turned out so well.

"Usual tonight, Mr. Shaw?"

Shaking his head, Max turned to the girl. "No. Let's have a beer, a light beer, a diet soda, and a sweet tea, please."

"Mixing things up. That's cool. Comin' right up."

Max leaned back on the counter as he waited for the order. Maybe Helene was right. Maybe it would have been better if they'd moved out of Glen Valley. Tonight, he was surrounded by people who'd known him for years, who made certain assumptions. Even the girl at the counter knew his usual order. He'd never questioned his choices before, but he also hadn't been so frustrated with his wife that he was actually considering ending his marriage.

He turned toward the clapping and shouting that broke out on lane fourteen. Pete pumped his arm in the air and waved to him.

"Got a strike! Hurry up with the beer!"

Max smiled.

Or maybe he was right where he was supposed to be.

7

"Tell me about this family tree project, Blake. When is it due?" Tasha said, running her hands through her hair. She hoped he hadn't waited until the last minute. She had done the same thing when she was in school, but now, as a parent, she knew what a bad idea that was. "What do you have to do?"

Blake looked up at her with chocolate frosting smeared across his face and shrugged.

"It's due Monday. Mrs. Anderson said we had all weekend to learn about our family for three generations. Our great-great-grandparents, plus cousins and stuff." He wiped his lips with the back of his hand, then licked the frosting from his arm. "Supposed to have pictures too."

Relieved with the three-day notice, Tasha relaxed until Libby began complaining.

"That's disgusting. Can't you eat like a normal person?" her daughter asked Blake as she brought the last bite of red velvet cake filled with chocolate mousse and topped with vanilla buttercream frosting to her mouth with a fork. "Like this."

Libby demonstrated the proper use of a utensil. In

response, Blake picked up the rest of the wedding cake sample on his plate and crammed it into his mouth. Crumbs and frosting fell to the table as he chewed with his mouth open.

Libby complained, "Mommy! Make him stop!"

Knowing the drill, Tasha grabbed a sponge from the sink and tossed it to Blake. "Use your manners and clean up your mess," she said. "Libby, he's just doing it to get a rise from you. Ignore him and he'll stop."

"I wish he'd go away." Libby picked up her plate, fork, and napkin and carried them to the sink. As she put the plate in the dishwasher, she said, "I think you should go with that one for the wedding cake. The chocolate filling is really good. Everybody would like it."

"White frosting's 'ucky. This cake is betta," Blake mumbled around the cake in his mouth. "Sides, Grandma's gonna pick what she likes, anyway."

Tasha took a deep breath. In the past, Blake might have been right, but that wasn't going to happen now.

"Blake, Greg and I will make decisions for our wedding. We will pick whatever we like. I am happy to hear your opinion, but ultimately, it's our choice. Not Grandma's. Not yours."

Blake shrugged. "If you say so." He picked up the sponge and smeared the cake on the table as he tried to get it on the plate. "Can you help me with the tree thing?"

"He should do it himself," Libby said. "I always do my homework by myself."

Knowing her daughter was right, Tasha let Libby march out of the kitchen before she turned to see Blake wiping the crumbs onto the floor.

"Stop that! You wipe into your hand, then dump the pieces in the trash can."

Her son looked up at her with his puppy dog eyes. "Will you help me?"

Shaking her head, she rolled her eyes. "If you can be a

messy eater, you can clean up. As far as your family tree project, I'll give you the lists I have. Libby used them when she made her family tree. You'll have to call your grandparents if you need anything else."

"I don't wanna call anyone."

"Well, you might not have to, but it's your project, and if you need something that isn't in my file, you'll have to get it."

Tasha remained still and waited. If she didn't teach Blake to do things for himself, he'd never grow up. Sure enough, he wiped the rest of the mess into his hand with the sponge and carefully walked to the sink. With his hands over the sink, he turned back to look at her.

"Can I dump them in here if I promise to rinse out the sink?"

With a proud nod, Tasha said, "Yes. That works too. Now, rinse the sponge, wring it out, and wipe off the table." When she was sure he was following instructions, she said, "I'll go get the list for you. Get your backpack and wait for me at the table."

She headed to the living room where she kept scrapbooks and reference materials for the kids. One thing she had learned as a single parent was that she had to know about both sides of the family. Her ex-husband was no help, nor were his parents. She'd relied on her ex-brother-in-law to fill in the gaps. Brad had provided an excellent resource on his family members going back seven generations on both sides. Blake would have no problem documenting his father's family tree.

Her side was a little more complicated.

Tasha pulled out a folder her dad had given her a few years ago. He'd discovered an online genealogy website and assembled a detailed list of everything he had learned. Although they'd all passed away, Tasha still remembered her dad's parents and grandparents from holidays and birthday celebrations when she'd been younger.

That wasn't the case with her mom's family. She couldn't remember meeting anyone related to her mother. Tasha had asked Sara about it at one point, but Sara didn't know either.

"Mom never brought it up. I even had to switch final projects in my high school sociology class."

"Oh. I always wondered what that was all about," said Tasha. "Didn't Mr. Biggins accuse you of being a better teacher than he was?"

Sara smiled. "There was that too. But he didn't believe me when I told him we had no information about Mom's family. He threatened to fail me."

"What happened?"

Sara shrugged. "I don't know. Mom went to school for a parent-teacher meeting, and after that, I got another project. No one told me why. When I asked, Mr. Biggins told me it had been worked out. When I pressed him, he said to ask Mom."

"Let me guess," Tasha said. "Mom refused to discuss it."

Sara nodded. "I asked Dad, but he said if she wanted to tell me, she would."

Pulling the single piece of paper out of the folder that contained information about Helene's family, Tasha blew her bangs out of her face. This would have to be enough information for Blake's tree because, if Helene didn't share the information with her daughters, why would she share it with her grandchildren?

"Mom!" Blake yelled from the kitchen. "I'm ready. Are you coming back?"

Tasha slid the file back in the cabinet and gathered the papers she'd pulled out. She knew the rest of her afternoon would be spent helping Blake understand the documents she had in her hand.

As she walked into the kitchen, Blake said, "Mrs. Anderson said I should make a separate tree for Greg's family. She knows you're getting married and said this would be something good for you to have if you decide to have another baby."

Tasha sighed. Funny how everyone in the community had ideas about her and Greg's new life. Not that it was any of their business. But right now, she needed to deal with the missing branches of the family trees.

"Okay, Blake. Let's get this project going."

8

Helene poured herself a bowl of high-fiber cereal. She had gained two pounds after drinking the two glasses of wine Thursday night, so she needed to compensate for the splurge. She poured a scant amount of almond milk in the bowl, grabbed her spoon, and sat down at the kitchen table.

The house was quiet. Max was still out of sorts about the uneaten eggplant Parmesan and tiramisu. She'd tried to explain it to him when he came home after work on Friday night, but he just shook his head and took his leftovers to the living room. When she'd woken up this morning, his side of the bed was already empty. He'd left her a note, letting her know he was working all weekend. Something about a special project he needed to have ready on Monday.

"He's avoiding me," she mumbled with her mouth full. "So be it. I've got more than enough to keep me busy."

She choked down the cereal, which tasted like cardboard, and skimmed her list of to-dos for the weekend. Bunco was Tuesday night. She'd signed up to bring a salad, so she needed to drop by Betty's Coffee Bar to get a few options. She could make something herself, but everyone loved Betty's homemade coleslaw, German potato salad, and artichoke-salami surprise.

The baker had given her a deadline of Wednesday to order a wedding cake. The crowns were due back at the bridal store on Friday.

Also looming on her calendar was the second appointment with Dr. Austen. They met again on Wednesday, and she still hadn't completed the assignment she was given. The incident in the cafeteria with Dorothy was a start, but Helene suspected the therapist would want more than a run-in with the school bully.

Crunching the last bit of cereal, Helene stood up to get a cup of coffee. She flipped the switch to heat up the single-serve coffee maker and selected a pod of her preferred dark roast. As she popped it into the machine, a memory of her daddy and his coffee came to mind.

"Oh, she'll have a field day with that," Helene said as she picked up the notebook she now thought of as her therapy journal. Tossing it on the table with a pen, she cleared her dishes and put them away before picking up her steaming mug of hot coffee.

She set the mug to the side as she flipped open the notebook to a fresh page and picked up her pen to write. As she wrote, she found herself back in her childhood home.

HELENE SAT at the red-and-white-checkered kitchen table, a plate of buttermilk pancakes sitting in front of her. A pad of real butter melted, mixing in with the sweet maple syrup that Mommy let her have on special occasions.

Orange juice waited for her in the glass emblazoned with green kitty cats. She liked them almost as much as she'd liked the blue bunny rabbits, but it had broken into a lot of pieces when Daddy threw it across the kitchen last week. Mommy said she'd find another one, but for now Helene had to make do with the kitties.

Mommy put a napkin in her lap. "Best not get syrup on that pretty dress of yours. As soon as we're finished, we're heading to Barney's for your picture."

Helene cut a small bite from her pancake like Mommy had taught her. She let the syrup drip off before she brought it to her mouth. As carefully as she could, she put the food in her mouth and chewed. Pancakes were her favorite food in the world, and Mommy's were the best.

After she wiped her face, Helene asked, "Last year, all of us got our picture taken. Why is it just me this year?"

She studied her mother's face while she waited for an answer. Mommy took a sip of her coffee before she answered.

"This year's for you, honey. When children are little, they change a lot every year. But when you get to be an adult like Daddy and me, you look the same. For the most part."

Helene saw Mommy look out the window above the sink. She knew her mother would stare outside for a minute, so Helene continued eating her pancakes. The plate was half empty before Helene saw her mother stiffen.

She sees Daddy, Helene thought, and her heart rate sped up. She looked down at her plate of food. With a quick glance back at her mother to make sure she wasn't paying attention, Helene picked up a pancake, ripped it in half, and shoved it in her mouth. If Daddy was in a bad mood when he came home, he'd send her away so he could eat in peace. She didn't know what that meant other than she wouldn't get to finish her beloved pancakes.

Wiping her hands on her napkin, Helene picked up her fork and returned to cutting the pancakes like expected, all the while keeping an eye on her mother.

Mommy sipped her coffee slowly, which was a good sign. That usually meant Daddy would be funny and nice and let

Helene sit at the table and finish her breakfast while he drank a cup of coffee.

The mornings Mommy poured her coffee down the drain were bad. Those usually happened on the days Daddy didn't come home before she went to bed, and he always complained about how he was going to be late for work that morning. He and Mommy fought and said mean things to each other.

Helene finished the last of her pancakes and bit into her bacon. She chewed as she looked for any sign of what to expect when Daddy entered the house. Using two hands, she picked up her orange juice and took three big sips. If there was any left when Daddy came in, he'd drink it, sometimes after adding his special drink from the big bottle in the bar.

She let out a sigh of relief when she saw Mommy take the brown bottle down from over the refrigerator. Mommy said it was dessert in a bottle and made coffee taste better. This was a sign that, when Daddy walked in the door, he would be happy.

Sure enough, when her father stumbled into the kitchen, he had a smile and a kiss for both Helene and her mother. Mommy poured him a cup of coffee and topped it off with the contents of the brown bottle. Helene wished he put cream or sugar in his coffee like Edith's daddy did, but at least she would get to finish her food.

"And what are you two doing today?" Daddy asked as he leaned back in the kitchen chair. "It's a nice day. How about we go to the swimming pool after I take myself a nap?"

Helene hopped out of her seat. "Daddy, I'm gettin' my picture taken today. Can we go after that?"

He leaned close to her, and she wrinkled her nose at his smell. She didn't know what it was, but he always smelled funny when he came home on mornings like this. As she pulled back, she noticed something red on his neck. She knew better than to say anything, though. Whenever she did,

Mommy would get sad and wake up with bruises on her arms the next day.

"You sure are high-maintenance for a little girl." Daddy took a swig of his coffee and nodded. "Yes, a boy would have been better. Your momma really messed that one up, didn't she?"

Helene bowed her head and stayed quiet. Sometimes, if she let Daddy talk, he forgot about her. She stayed where she was until she heard Daddy's soft snores. Then she looked up and over at Mommy.

"Can we go get my picture taken now?"

Mommy carefully took the coffee cup out of Daddy's hand and set it on the table. She put a finger to her lips to remind Helene to be quiet and nodded her head. As quietly as they could, mother and daughter left the house for the short walk to the portrait studio.

It only took a few minutes to arrive, but there was a short line waiting ahead of them.

"Do you think we have time for the picture? I don't want to miss the swimming pool."

Her mother lit a cigarette and nodded. "We'll be fine. I'm not sure Daddy will be up for a trip to the pool when he wakes up."

Helene tried not to let the prospect of a cancelled pool visit upset her, but when it was her turn to get her picture taken, it took the photographer, Mr. Barney, four tries to coax a smile to her face.

"What's wrong with you, Helene? You're usually all smiles and giggles," said Mr. Barney. "I can't charge your momma for a portrait if you're frowning."

She looked over at her mother, who was chatting with Edith's mommy and blowing smoke rings over the top of her head. Wanting to make Mommy happy and get her trip to the pool, Helene summoned up her remaining energy and plastered a smile on her face.

"There it is! I knew you could do better!" Mr. Barney shot a few more pictures, then walked over to where Helene was sitting. He helped her down and gave her a lollipop before turning to the next child in line.

Helene took her mother's hand, and they walked around town, completing the rest of their errands. They got home a few hours later. Helene ran straight to her room to get changed for the pool, but when she hurried to the kitchen in her swim costume, Daddy's snores greeted her.

"I'm sorry, honey. Daddy's not ready for a trip to the pool," Mommy said softly. "We'll try again tomorrow. Now, you go change your clothes. You can play in your room or outside. Just be quiet."

SATISFIED YET SAD about the journal entry she'd written, Helene absently grabbed her coffee and sipped. The cold liquid startled her, and she glanced up at the clock. Surprised to see she'd been at the table for almost an hour, she picked up her therapy journal and her half-full mug of cold coffee. Scolding herself for the waste, she dumped the coffee into the sink and put the mug in the dishwasher. She tucked the journal in her purse before heading to her bedroom to get ready for the rest of her day.

Shaking off the gloom that remained from her trip down memory lane, Helene decided it would be best to see Tasha face-to-face about the cake and the crowns. And, since she was out, she would include a trip by Max's office. She was mad at him for making her do this therapy, but that didn't mean she didn't miss his company.

9

Double-checking that the bridal crowns were in the pink shopping bag, Helene slid out of her car and headed toward Tasha's porch. She hadn't bothered to call. If she had let her daughter know she was coming by, Tasha might have put up some excuse or even left for a bit. Helene knew how her daughters reacted to her.

But a surprise drop-in with the premise of following up on the cakes and just happening to have the crowns in her car was the perfect setup.

As she walked up the porch steps, she stepped over her grandson's scooter. "That's a hazard if I've ever seen one," Helene said, and added it to the mental list of things to discuss with her daughter. She rang the doorbell and glanced at her reflection in the window. All looked well.

Footsteps pounded toward the door, and Helene prepared herself for a boisterous welcome from Blake. The door flung open. But instead of a warm greeting, Blake frowned at her.

"How come you won't tell Mommy about your parents?"

Taken aback by the comment, Helene didn't know what to say. It seemed like too much of a coincidence that Blake was asking about her parents and Dr. Austen was forcing her to write about them too. Struggling to regain her composure, Helene held out her arms.

"What about a hug for your grandma?"

Blake stood there for a minute before he moved closer.

"Stop!" Tasha's voice carried out to the porch where Helene was standing. "Do not hug him unless you want glue all over your clothes!"

Helene sidestepped her grandson's arms. She carefully put the bag with the crowns on the porch. She took Blake's shoulders in her hands and squeezed.

"I think that'll have to do until we make sure you're clean." She glanced down at her sundress. "We wouldn't want to ruin this pretty dress, now, would we? It's Grandpa's favorite."

Max hated this dress, but that was beside the point. She still needed to stop at the store and by Max's office. She didn't have time to get home and change before she finished the rest of her errands.

Blake shook his head. "Whatever. But I have to know 'bout your parents or I'll fail my family tree homework."

Without waiting for her response, Blake took off down the hallway. Helene picked up the bag and followed, closing the door behind her. She headed to the kitchen where she knew Blake did his homework A quick glance into the living room told her Tasha's clean streak had continued.

Good for her. A tidy house makes for a better start to this marriage.

"Hello!" she called out as she entered the kitchen. Sure enough, Blake stood next to the kitchen table where his backpack, a stack of papers, and a pile of craft supplies rested. While she wanted to tell her daughter and grandson how many germs were on a backpack and why it shouldn't be on the kitchen table, she asked instead, "What's this I hear about a family tree?"

Tasha looked up at her mother with what Helene could only call irritation. Before her daughter could explain, Helene put up her hand. "Not this again. I have a right to privacy, you know." She set her bags on the floor next to the table. "Besides, why is it necessary to have children do this project every single year?"

Her daughter dropped her face into her hands.

"You know, you'll get wrinkles and blemishes if you touch your face," Helene admonished.

Blake frowned at her. "What's a blemish?"

Before Helene could answer, Libby skipped into the room.

"It's a zit." She put her arms around Helene and gave her a hug before she peeked into the pink bag. "What's that?"

Helene leaned down and pulled out several tissue-wrapped crowns. "Something for your mother's wedding. We didn't get a chance to talk about them when she taste-tested cakes the other day." Holding the crowns in her hand, Helene asked, "What did you two think of the cakes I sent home with your mother?"

Libby shrugged. "I like the donuts Mommy brought home better."

Blake shook his head. "Not me. The chocolate cake was the best."

Giving her daughter a triumphant look, Helene handed Libby a crown. "You can unwrap that. Be careful, though."

"What about me?" Blake put his hands out. "I wanna unwrap something."

Helene shook her head. "This is something for girls only. I'll have something for you some other time." She nodded at the stuff on the table. "Besides, you're supposed to be doing your homework."

Tasha leaned back in the chair and crossed her arms. "Which he can't do because he doesn't have your family tree information."

Helene's jaw clenched. Leave it to Tasha to badger her about something as silly as her parents. Rather than address her daughter, she focused on Libby's reaction to the sparkling tiara she was balancing on her head.

"Do you like it?" Helene asked, although she could tell from the awe in her granddaughter's eyes that she loved it. "That one is a little big for you, but I have some others that might work."

"Mom, we discussed this. I'm not wearing a crown for the wedding. It's not my style. I thought we agreed."

Helene nodded as she watched Libby twirl around in circles, careful to keep the rhinestone-studded creation centered on her head.

"That doesn't mean Libby can't wear one. All girls want to be princesses. This would be fun for her."

"Kings wear crowns too," said Blake, and he dove toward the bag. He grabbed a piece of tissue paper before Helene could push the bag out of his reach.

"Young man, you have glue on your hands. If you touch a crown with glue, what do you think will happen?"

Blake shook his hand, but the tissue paper stuck to it. He pulled the paper with his other hand, but instead of removing it, the tissue ripped, leaving paper stuck to both his hands.

"I dunno," he said as he flapped his hands around, the tissue paper trailing in the breeze. "What do I do now?"

Libby laughed. "You look silly! I bet your soccer friends would love a picture of you flapping around." Libby ran over to the kitchen counter to grab her mother's phone. "Can I take a picture of him, Mommy? We can show Greg when he comes by later."

Blake's faced flushed red. "No way! That's not fair. You don't like it when I take pictures of you."

The kids continued to argue back and forth, and Helene pointed at her daughter.

"Aren't you going to do something about that?" From the

relaxed look on her daughter's face and the fact that Tasha didn't move from her chair, something told Helene that Tasha was going to let the argument play out. "If you don't, I will."

"No, Mom, you won't. Truth be told, you started this argument. I told you I didn't want a crown, yet here you are, dropping by on a Saturday morning with an entire bag of them." Tasha nodded at the table. "But since you're here, and if you want to be helpful, can you give me something for this family tree project? Libby made it through hers because it was about the same time her dad ended up in the hospital, and the teacher took pity on her. But Blake doesn't have an excuse."

Helene looked from her daughter to her grandchildren. Libby was running around the table, always a few steps ahead of her brother, whose hands resembled peacock tails. Sighing her displeasure, Helene nodded. She could make up some story that would be good enough for a third grader.

"Fine. Get them to stop yelling and I'll help Blake with the project."

Tasha's eyes narrowed. "Are you telling me the truth or what I want to hear? Because I'm not stopping *this*," she tilted her head at her kids, "if you aren't really going to help with *that*," and she tilted her head toward the backpack.

Why is everyone being so difficult lately? Deciding to deal with matters herself, Helene clapped her hands to get her grandchildren's attention. "Blake and Libby! Stop immediately."

The kids continued to argue, and Helene repeated her request two more times before looking at Tasha.

"What's going on here? Why aren't they listening to me?"

Tasha's eyebrows went up. "They're ignoring you."

Glaring at her daughter, Helene asked, "Why is that?"

"Because I don't think they believe you anymore than I do."

Indignation ripped through Helene. "I don't have to take this. I have better things to do than help you with your wedding—"

"Which I never asked you to do."

"Or work on a silly grade-school homework assignment—"

"Which you could easily do if you would just tell me about your parents."

Throwing her hands into the air, Helene shouted, "Fine. You win!"

As soon as the words were out of her mouth, Libby and Blake stopped arguing.

"What did I win?" asked Blake.

Libby shook her head. "She meant *I* won."

"Stop. Both of you," Tasha said. "Libby, take off the crown, wrap it back up, and go back to your room. Blake, come here."

Helene's granddaughter did as she was told, handed the crown back to Helene, and skipped out of the room. Helene tucked the crown back in the bag while Tasha pulled the tissue paper off Blake's hands, then sent him to the bathroom to wash off the glue.

"Now, before he gets back, what are you going to tell him about his great-grandparents? Seeing as I don't even know their names, I'm kinda curious too."

Panic started up Helene's neck. She didn't understand why the mere mention of her parents made her panic, but a hot flash threatened to overwhelm her, and she stumbled to a chair.

"Mom, what's wrong?" Tasha's voice sounded like it was coming from someplace far away. Helene struggled to understand what she was saying. "Are you sick? Or is this just a way to avoid telling me about my grandparents?"

Helene felt her heart pounding in her chest as she gasped for more air. "Water, please," was all that came out.

The room got dark, and she forced herself to focus on her breathing. In and out.

Relax. This is getting out of control, and it's all Dr. Austen's fault.

If she hadn't made me remember so much about my parents, I'd be handling this much better.

Tasha shoved a glass of water into her hand. "Drink this. Slowly, though. You look like you've seen a ghost."

Taking small sips, Helene regained control of herself. Her breathing slowed, and the hot flash passed. Her heart rate was slowing, though it was still faster than normal. She needed to get out of here. There was no way she could tell her daughter or grandchildren about Doris and Glenn in this state.

Helene inhaled deeply and smiled at her daughter. Thinking fast, she came up with the most obvious excuse she could think of. "Sorry about that. I've been having some issues lately. The doctor is working on regulating my hormones, but, as you can see, it isn't working yet."

Tasha's brows pulled together. If she'd felt better, Helene would have reminded her that frowning created wrinkles. Instead, she finished off the glass of water and placed it on the table.

"I need to go home. The doctor said, if this happened, I should rest."

Her daughter's hand stopped her. "Are you sure you can drive?"

Nodding, Helene said, "I'll be fine. I'm going straight home." *Via Max's office, but no need to tell you that.*

At first, she didn't think Tasha believed her, but her daughter gathered her things and helped her take them to the car. Helene started the car, and Tasha said, "Call me when you get home, please. I'm worried."

Irritated by her daughter's sudden interest in her well-being, Helene nodded and closed the car door. With a quick wave, she backed out of the driveway and headed in the direction of her house.

She drove mindlessly for a few minutes to calm down. It

would make matters worse if she showed up at Max's office this upset.

"Stupid school projects," she muttered.

Flipping on the radio, she found a smooth jazz station and willed herself to relax. After a few more deep breaths, Helene turned the car toward Max. She vowed that something good was going to happen today. If it killed her.

10

"And he's done it again. The third green jacket for this scandal-ridden golfer. Let's hope this year doesn't end as last year did."

Max minimized his Internet browser while in agreement with the sportscaster. He'd decided to spend his weekend in the office, away from Helene, because he was still irritated about her refusal of his dinner. And he couldn't eat any more leftover eggplant Parmesan. It was good, but only for a few days.

He also knew she wouldn't do her therapy work if he was in the house. Every time he walked through the kitchen, she flipped the notebook she was writing in closed. Max didn't blame her. He wouldn't be comfortable sharing his feelings with a perfect stranger.

But the stranger was also a therapist whom he had picked to help get their lives back on track. Dr. Austen came highly recommended. Being located in a town several miles away helped as well. All her professional credentials were in place, and she had her own monthly column in the county magazine. All these things should have made Helene happy, but she didn't acknowledge any of it.

Max scratched his head. Spending the weekend at the office wasn't helping the situation, but he didn't know what else to do. She needed to relax and stop dictating everyone's lives to them, including his.

To distract himself, he pulled up his email and began addressing issues that could wait until Monday. It didn't take long for him to clear the entire mailbox.

"Who knew I'd get to Inbox Zero?"

Pushing away from his desk, he walked to the window and looked out. The parking lot was empty, except for his car and the security guard's. He remembered the days when the lot was full twenty-four-seven. The economy hadn't been kind to the engineering firm, but the firm had managed to support his family through the years. He and Helene had bought the house, joined the country club, paid for the girls' college educations. He wished he could have paid for Sara's law school degree, but she'd insisted on covering that herself, much to her mother's chagrin.

In retrospect, he figured it was probably to show her mother that she could make it on her own. Helene's relationships with her daughters had always been tense, but with Sara, things got out of control quickly.

He meant to ask Dr. Austen if that was because Helene had lost her mother so young. She hadn't had the same kind of bond with her grandmother that she would have had with her mother. Max thought that could be part of the problem.

But he didn't think that was the only reason. If it were, then Helene would have gladly taken him up on his offer to travel the world when they became empty nesters. They could have seen all the places Helene had dreamed of when they were first married: New York City, Chicago, London, Sydney.

Now that they could travel, Helene was hell-bent on getting her own way in a town she swore she hated. She never wanted to leave for fear of missing a committee meeting or a Bunco game or some other issue that really didn't matter as far as he was concerned.

It was like she was afraid to take the opportunities he had worked so hard to provide for her. And, in the meantime, she continued to drive everyone away.

As he continued to gaze at the parking lot, Helene's car pulled into the spot next to his. Surprised, he walked to his desk and checked his phone for missed calls or texts. Nothing.

Worried that something might be wrong, he hurried to the reception area where Stan, the weekend security guard, sat.

"I didn't know your wife was coming by today."

Knowing that, the last time Stan saw Helene, she had berated him for wearing a brown belt with black shoes, he nodded.

"I'll take her straight to my office. You don't need a fashion intervention again."

Chuckling, Stan said as he stood up, "That's okay. I wore the black belt today. But since you're here to let her in, I'm going to do my rounds." He turned and headed down the hallway.

Glad that Stan didn't hold a grudge but not surprised he didn't want to talk to his wife, Max opened the front door for Helene. A quick appraisal told him something was off, but he knew better than to ask what the matter was. She'd tell him if she wanted to. Asking only aggravated her.

"This is a surprise. I didn't expect to see you here today." He leaned in to give her a kiss and was surprised at her response. She leaned into him and wrapped her arms around his neck. He hugged her back, enjoying the sudden show of affection, but was confused at the same time. After a minute, he gently pushed her back and looked into her eyes. "What was that for?"

"Can we talk in your office?" Helene didn't wait for an answer. She took his hand and pulled him down the hall.

Rather than ask questions, Max followed. He closed the door behind them, in case Stan got curious, and watched as Helene made herself comfortable on his couch.

"Did you get your work done today?" Max heard a slight tremor in his wife's voice, telling him she was nervous. "You didn't say what you were doing."

Between that and the hug, Max braced himself for bad news. He joined his wife on the couch and reached for her hand. "I did. But that's not why you're here. What's going on?"

She squeezed his hand before dropping it, standing up, and walking to the window. Helene looked out, and he followed her gaze.

"You saw me pull up, didn't you?"

"Yes."

"Because I saw you standing at the window." She walked to his desk and looked at it. She nodded at his spotless workspace as she crossed her arms over her chest. "Why did you come to the office today? It wasn't to do work, that's for sure."

Counting to ten as Dr. Austen had recommended, Max gave himself time to process before he responded. He debated how much of the truth he should tell her and decided he might as well put his cards on the table.

"I wanted to give you space."

Helene dropped into the chair behind the desk. She didn't say anything as she spread her hands on the desk blotter and looked around the room. "Space for what?"

Not sure if she was making this difficult or if she really didn't know, Max forced himself to relax on the sofa. "Space for you to do your homework for Dr. Austen." She stiffened at the therapist's name, but he continued. "We got off to a bad start last week, and I thought dinner was a good idea—"

"Except I'm dieting."

"Except you're dieting." He held up his hands in surrender.

"I know that now. You also know that I think dieting is ridiculous and I love you the way you are. There's no reason to change."

He regretted the words the instant they came out of his mouth.

"Then why are we going to a therapist?"

Sighing, he shook his head. "Hold on. You know what I mean. We've talked about it before. I want the woman I married thirty-seven years ago back. The person you've become the last few years isn't what I signed up for. I'm not asking you to change into someone else or lose a bunch of weight or significantly alter your moral compass. I just want the woman I fell in love with. Is that too much to ask?"

Helene stood up and brushed imaginary lint from her slacks. "I came by to see if you wanted to go out to dinner with me. My apology for being late on Wednesday night. But it's clear that you aren't interested in me. You're stuck in the past, and this therapy thing is a ploy to get me to change."

"That's not true at all. I want my wife back. My family back. Something's wrong and you won't admit it. You're worried about something right now, and I don't know what it is because you won't tell me. Be mad at me for the therapy if you want, but I wouldn't fight for this if I didn't mean it."

For a minute, neither of them spoke, and hope burned in Max's chest. All she needed to do was give him a hint, a glimmer of what was going on inside her right now, and he would be happy. But he didn't know if he could take Helene's denial. Refusing to see the truth wasn't helping anyone.

When she didn't speak, he tried again. "Why are you really here?"

She rolled her eyes, a sure sign she was hiding something. "I came by to find out why you were here, which I have successfully done, and now I can go about the rest of my day."

Helene picked up her purse and started toward the door when Max said, "I don't believe you. It's something else. You don't hug me like that if there isn't something bothering you."

He could see the internal struggle in her eyes. He held his breath as he waited. Would she trust him, or was this going to be another wasted conversation?

Max let out his breath as Helene returned to the couch and sat down.

"I'm not sure if I love or hate the fact that you know me so well."

He waited, knowing if he interrupted Helene might clam up again.

"I went to Tasha's house." Before he could chastise her, she held up her hands. "I know, I know. Stupid thing to do. But I had to try again on the crowns. She doesn't understand how much better she'll look if she just gives them a chance."

Irritated that Helene continued to harass their daughter, Max got up. Helene's hand shot out and pulled him back down.

"Wait. Hear me out."

"There's more?" Max asked, half-standing. "I'm not sure I want to know."

"Blake has a family tree project. Tasha asked me about my parents. I panicked as I used to when we were first married."

Max remembered his anxiety when his new wife had lost the color in her face or fainted.

"I didn't know it still bothered you," said Max.

Helene shrugged and said in a raspy voice, "It doesn't anymore. Or didn't until Dr. Austen started asking questions. I scared Tasha, though. She wanted me to go straight home, but I couldn't be alone. I needed to be with someone who understands."

She let go of his hands and buried her face in her own. Helene's back shook as she sobbed. Max hugged her toward him, finally understanding the purpose behind her visit. As he waited for her to calm down, he wondered if forcing her to see a therapist was the right thing to do.

11

Checking her makeup in the overhead mirror, Helene frowned when she noticed the red bags under her eyes. Her crying fit with Max on Saturday had started a trend. Sunday and Monday she had found herself leaking tears of misery. It galled her that her parents, who had been dead for fifty years, still had the power to make her cry.

"At least Max didn't see me cry again." She'd made sure she kept a smile on her face to mask her sadness. At least until he left for work Monday morning. Then she'd let the waterworks flow.

Except today, she didn't have time to deal with it. Tuesday was Bunco, and she had to get her salads picked up from Betty's Coffee Bar. She couldn't walk into a public place with any evidence of weakness. She considered Betty a friend, but you could never be too careful about who else might be in the store.

She gently tapped more concealer under each eye, set it with some powder, and checked her image again. "Much better." Helene added a little color to her lips and decided she looked almost normal. If anyone asked, she'd say she'd been fighting a migraine. That was close enough to the truth.

Helene surveyed the parking lot. She recognized a few cars, but she wasn't concerned with any of their owners. She knew how to handle the people inside.

As she glided in the door, she surveyed her surroundings. The men's Bible study group sat around a table topped with coffee and donuts. A young mother helped her toddlers pick out treats from the display case. Helene took her place in line, close enough to the counter that Betty would see her but far enough away that one of the toddlers wouldn't accidentally touch her with their dirty hands. She loved children, especially her grandchildren, but dirty hands on linen pants were the worst.

"Morning, Helene," Betty called out as she deposited the blue-and-green-sprinkled donut the little boy pointed at into a bag. She waited for his sister to make her selection. "You here for salads? It's Bunco night."

Nodding in agreement, Helene said, "I'd like to do a variety this week."

Before she could continue, Betty put her hand up to signal, "Hold on." She leaned forward to see the little girl's choice and pulled out a pink-frosted sugar cookie with white sprinkles. The little girl nodded and leaned her head against her mother's leg.

The image jolted Helene. She didn't know when or where, but she knew she'd done the same thing to her mother when she was a child.

It's that therapist's fault I remember.

Wrapping her arms around herself, Helene attempted to stop the shivering the image triggered. Her body stilled by the time Betty rang up the children's purchases. Pleased she'd gotten a hold of herself, she put a pleasant expression on her face as Betty turned back to the case and pointed at each salad as she spoke.

"I've got the mustard potato salad, a BLT pasta salad, and

coleslaw ready now," said Betty, her elbows up on the counter. "I'm behind schedule, so the German potato salad won't be ready until after four. What would you like?"

Helene felt tears threaten to spill again. *Oh my god. I'm crying over potato salad. Dr. Austen is a complete quack.*

She concentrated on the case in hopes that Betty didn't notice her discomfort.

"The coleslaw for sure. I was hoping for the German salad and the artichoke-salami surprise. You could bring those with you tonight when you come, couldn't you?"

When Betty didn't respond, Helene took her eyes off the counter and glanced up. Betty stared at her, shaking her head.

"What's wrong?" Helene asked. "You've taken food with you before."

"It's not the food," said Betty. "What in the world is wrong with you?"

Not wanting to admit anything, Helene's eyebrows flew up. "Nothing. I'm picking up food. Is there something wrong with that?"

Before Helene know what was happening, Betty walked around the counter, took hold of Helene's arm, and dragged her through the door marked "Employees Only." Betty dropped her arm and stood facing her, her arms crossed over her chest and a frown plastered on her face.

"Do not mention food to me again until you tell me the truth. Why have you been crying? And don't bother telling me it's because I don't have German potato salad."

Helene swallowed back her tears. "It's Tasha. She is being difficult about the wedding."

Instead of the sympathy she expected, Betty snarled.

"That's crap and you know it. You might be able to sell that to the therapist you're seeing, but not me. Tell me the truth or, so help me, I will not make any salads for you today."

Helene gasped. "You're the only person who could say that to me, you know?"

Betty nodded. "And I'm probably the only person other than Max who really cares that you're lying through your veneers." She paused. Helene felt Betty's eyes searching her own. "Aren't you going to ask how I found out about the therapist?"

"Max told you, obviously."

Taking a seat on a stool, Betty said, "Do you know why he told me?"

Tired of all the questions, Helene shifted her weight from one kitten heel to the other.

"No, but I'm sure you're about to tell me."

Helene jumped as Betty's hand slapped down on her thigh. Betty's patience level was high, but she had pushed her friend too far.

With a grim smile, Betty said, "Glad I got your attention, because someone needs to straighten you out. I'll be damned if you won't listen to Max or the therapist. I've seen you do a lot of rotten things over the years, but lately, you've exceeded everyone's expectations."

Helene clasped her hands together behind her back so Betty wouldn't see her twisting her wedding ring. "Really? What exactly are you referring to?"

"Don't play stupid. You and I both know you need to take this seriously. Max isn't putting up with it anymore. He's already lost one daughter because of you, and you're in the process of alienating a second one."

"That's not true. Sara had a better job opportunity, and she took it. It had nothing to do with me."

Betty stood up and walked toward the door. "Lying to yourself is one thing. Lying to a friend is something else." She turned back toward Helene. "I'll bring the salads tonight, but this is the last time I'm serving you until you figure out whatever your problem is. And don't bother making small talk with me at Bunco. I've had enough of you for now."

Before Helene could protest, Betty left the room.

12

True to her word, Betty delivered the salads to Bunco at Cybil Anderson's house that night. Helene thanked her and paid for the food, but after that, Betty steered clear of her.

Helene noticed the group was quieter than usual during the dinner portion of the evening. Despite the excellent salads she had contributed, no one complimented her. Everyone told Betty what a great job she did on the side dishes while Helene fumed that she got no recognition for ordering them.

Even when she regaled the group with stories of Sara in Chicago, no one responded. She didn't think anyone knew she'd made up the tale of Sara meeting the director of the aquarium and getting free admission for life. But usually she got some sort of reaction from the group.

Things didn't get any better during the game itself. Going into the final round of the last set, Helene found herself at table four with Betty, Cybil, and Renee, the receptionist at Sara's old law firm. She and Renee sat across from each other, making them partners. Knowing what a gabber Renee was, Helene assumed her luck had turned.

It hadn't.

"Sara didn't mention anything to me about the aquarium when I talked to her this week," Renee said as they waited for Cybil to roll the dice. "In fact, she didn't mention that she talked to you at all."

Helene realized her error, but it was too late to do anything about it. Usually, Renee updated her earlier in the evening with whatever it was Sara wanted her to know, but tonight Renee had been strangely quiet. She'd assumed that meant Renee and Sara hadn't talked, but she was wrong.

Helene caught the look that passed between Cybil and Betty. Normally, she could count on Betty to have her back, but after this morning's discussion, Helene knew she was on her own.

Clearing her throat, Helene said, "I'm sure she was busy and just forgot about it."

Renee shook her head. "I don't know. Ever since she moved to Chicago, she's been more driven and focused than I've seen her in a long time. Are you sure she mentioned the aquarium?"

Just then, Cybil finished her turn and passed the dice to Helene. Thankful for the diversion, Helene rolled the dice, hoping for at least one six. Instead, she got a two, four, and five, which Betty quickly snatched up.

"My turn," Betty said, and rolled.

Renee persisted. "Sara doesn't forget things like that, especially since Tasha is flying there with the kids in a few weeks. Sara planned a great visit for them. Interestingly enough, they are going to the aquarium."

Realizing Renee wasn't any help, Helene turned to Cybil. "How's school going? My grandson says you give out a lot of homework."

The words were barely out of her mouth when she remembered Cybil was the teacher who had assigned Blake's ridiculous family tree project. Before she could decide how to cover her second mistake of the evening, Betty yelled, "Bunco!"

A chorus of groans and cheers filled the room at the sudden end of the game. Everyone at the table added up their scores, and Renee offered to take the scorecards to the head table. Betty went with her, leaving Helene alone with Cybil.

Looking around for a way to escape, she was out of luck when Cybil said, "School's fine." She paused before adding, "I noticed you didn't help Blake with his family tree project."

Helene kept her eyes focused on her manicure while she said, "That's not really my responsibility. His mother is more than capable of helping him. Besides . . ." She glanced up and noticed several people at the table next to theirs, listening intently. Squirming in her seat, she cleared her throat before continuing. "Besides, I wouldn't be any help. It is his project, after all."

Uncomfortable with the direction the conversation was heading, Helene pushed back from the table. She had no intention of explaining herself to the group. "I have an early start tomorrow." She looked over to Cybil. "Thanks for hosting Bunco this evening. Sorry to leave so early."

She'd made it all the way to the front door when someone called her name.

"You forgot your prize," said Cybil, holding out a pink gift bag with turquoise tissue paper sticking out the top. "You were the night's biggest loser. I've never seen anyone lose seventeen out of eighteen rounds. That's unheard of."

Helene yanked the sack out of Cybil's hand and hustled down the sidewalk. Voices floated out the window as she walked away from the house.

"How can anyone be that callous? Not wanting to help her grandson. Serves her right to lose tonight."

"I heard she hasn't talked to Sara in months. Her daughter had to leave town because of her."

"My Frank said Max could barely keep up at bowling last week. His mind was somewhere else."

As fast as she could, Helene hurried to her car. She turned on the engine and eased away from the curb. She drove several blocks, far enough away from Cybil's house that no one would see her, and pulled alongside the curb.

Tears of embarrassment and anger streaked down her face. When would this misery end? Everything had been fine until Max dragged her to the therapist, and now her past was popping up everywhere. She couldn't even have a night out with her friends without dealing with it.

"Friends" might not be the right term for the group tonight. "Acquaintances" seemed more fitting but equally depressing.

In frustration, she hit the steering wheel with her hand and immediately regretted it. Hitting things was never her MO. That was her father. Pain stabbed through her hand and her heart as another memory of her father came to mind. She fought it back, knowing now was not a good time to relive something she'd repressed for decades. She needed to get home.

Sucking in air to put out the fire that blazed in her chest, Helene rested her head on the steering wheel for a few moments. "I don't have time for this. I don't want to remember."

After a few minutes of deep breathing, Helene sat up. She'd wallowed enough. She needed to save this for the therapist. Dr. Austen would have a field day with all this in the morning.

13

Helene slept terribly after the debacle of the Bunco game. She'd been hoping for a good night's sleep so she could meet the therapist at her best, but her head throbbed, and her hand shook as she pushed open Dr. Austen's lobby door.

Today's appointment was between her and the therapist. She'd balked at the thought, but Max had insisted.

"I've been going alone for a few months. You were there by yourself last week."

Helene argued, "That was different. You went with me and then left. What am I supposed to say to this woman?"

"Start with hello. Then answer her questions." Max had gently kissed her cheek. "You told me you want someone to help you understand why you react the way you do about your family. Dr. Austen can do that. You have to let her."

Helene sank down onto the brown leather sofa to wait for her appointment. Dr. Austen's office door was closed, and quiet voices drifted into the lobby. To distract herself, Helene pulled out the notebook in which she was keeping all of Tasha's wedding information. Flipping to the to-do list, she skimmed through it, marking things off here and there.

She added an asterisk next to the all-important *Select a Dress* item. She couldn't convince Tasha to join her at Darci's Wedding Barn. Eight dresses were waiting for Tasha to try on, but her daughter insisted she was wearing something she'd ordered from a retail chain store. And it wasn't even a wedding gown. It resembled a white tent that tied in the back.

She shook her head. If Tasha didn't get over her need to do everything by herself, this wedding would never get a write-up in *The Gazette*. The local paper's feature, "The Wedding of the Year," was at stake, and Helene had every intention of grabbing the distinction. Helene hadn't won the honor when she and Max got married, but there was nothing stopping her from achieving the pinnacle of wedding success this time around.

The office door opened, and Helene twisted in her seat to avoid being noticed. She kept her eyes glued to the notebook until she was sure the previous client had passed her. She didn't want anyone to see her. The office was out of town, so no one should recognize her, but she couldn't take any chances. On the other hand, curiosity made her peek as the person headed toward the door.

She recognized the fake Birkin bag the woman was carrying and choked back a giggle. What in the world was Eveline Gerome doing here? Despite not wanting to be noticed, there was no way Helene would let Tasha's ex-mother-in-law out of here without making it clear she'd been seen. Eveline judged Helene for everything she did, including Tasha's divorce from her son, Doug, even though he was a cheater.

Fixing a smile on her face, Helene called out, "Eveline! So nice to see you. Whatever are you doing here?"

The other woman stopped in her tracks. Helene wondered if she would turn around or keep marching out the door. Politeness apparently won out, because Eveline turned and pursed her lips.

"Same thing you are, Helene. Don't even think about spreading any gossip. It won't work."

Without another word, Eveline strode out the lobby door and slammed it behind her.

Helene turned back and saw Dr. Austen observing her. Unlike any normal person, Dr. Austen didn't wither at the look Helene gave her. The therapist just waved her into the room.

"I'm ready for you," she said, and turned back into her office.

Surprised at Dr. Austen's lack of response, Helene gathered her things. A surge of power went through her at the thought of having something over Eveline, and Helene sauntered into the office. She looked around to see if she could tell where Eveline had been sitting. An imprinted seat cushion on the couch gave away her predecessor's location, and Helene chose a seat at the other end.

Dr. Austen settled herself into a chair opposite the couch and picked up a leather portfolio. Helene glimpsed the gilded initials on the cover and laughed.

"Care to share the joke?" Dr. Austen asked.

Helene suspected the therapist wouldn't appreciate the fact that her initials were the same as the round green vegetable Helene despised, so she shook her head. "Just thinking about your previous patient." Knowing the therapist couldn't say anything due to HIPPA, Helene relaxed into her seat.

Nodding slowly, Dr. Austen's lips tipped up into a slight smile. "That's good. I thought you were going to comment on my portfolio." The therapist tilted it up so Helene could get a good look at the initials. "Most of my patients can't help themselves. PEA really is an unfortunate monogram."

Squirming in her seat, Helene shook her head. "Nothing

funny about a monogram." She nodded toward the portfolio. "I haven't seen one done like that before. It's lovely."

She watched Dr. Austen, assessing whether the therapist was going to press the subject or not. Helene didn't relax until Dr. Austen set the portfolio on her lap and pulled out her pen.

"So, did you get your assignment finished this week?" Glancing down at her notes, Dr. Austen said, "I believe you were to write about something in your childhood that made you uncomfortable. What did you come up with?"

Helene dug her therapy journal out of her handbag and handed it to Dr. Austen. The book remained in midair as Dr. Austen's hands stayed folded on her portfolio.

"I prefer to have my patients read their notes aloud. It's helpful to hear the experience in your words rather than mine."

"Of course," Helene said, adding under her breath, "It's a special kind of torture."

"Pardon?" Dr. Austen asked.

Shaking her head, Helene said, "It would be my honor."

Helene read aloud her lunchroom incident with Dorothy with as little emotion as possible. She was glad she'd picked this to write about. It was a mild memory in the scheme of things, and she made it through the account quickly and without emotion.

When she was finished, she looked up, expecting to be congratulated for her good work. Instead, Dr. Austen frowned at her.

"Is something wrong?" Helene asked.

"This doesn't sound like you at all. From what your husband has shared with me and from what I just observed in my lobby, you have no problem telling people how you feel. Whether they want to know or not." She jotted a few notes in her portfolio before continuing. "Plus, I gave you a week, and the best you came up with was an elementary school bullying incident. I expected more from you, to be honest."

Shocked at the woman's bluntness, Helene sat up ramrod straight and prepared her attack. "It was junior high. And I didn't think you could comment on other patients."

Dr. Austen raised her head and caught Helene's gaze. "Do you really think I'm going to violate HIPPA? My comment is based on the observation I made as you interacted with a complete stranger in my lobby. You wanted that woman to feel inferior to you. I don't need to be a PhD in marriage and family counseling to know when someone is trying to intimidate someone else."

Helene's heart thumped. "How dare you talk to me like that?"

"Are you telling me I'm wrong?"

Clenching her teeth, Helene considered her options. Max had hired this woman to get their marriage back on track. That was a bad sign. But so were the facts that Tasha had sabotaged the wedding plans she'd made, Bunco was a complete failure, and everyone thought she was a bad grandmother.

Since things weren't going well on her terms, maybe she should try something new. But it was years too late to come clean about the fact her parents had died because of her.

Helene stared back at Dr. Austen. She disliked the woman, but for whatever reason, Max thought the therapist could help. In a way, Dr. Austen sounded like Grammy. "Tough love" was what her grandmother used to call it. This was like "tough therapy."

Rubbing her fingers over her wedding ring, Helene willed herself to relax. If she continued to grind her teeth, she'd end up with a headache, and she didn't think stretching out on the couch would impress Dr. Austen, despite what she saw in the movies.

Helene gave in. "What were you expecting from me? I followed the directions on the sheet you gave me."

Dr. Austen tapped her pen against the portfolio. "I suppose.

But really? Someone pushed you into the school bully and she got covered in food? You didn't even get in trouble. The principal gave you lunch." She frowned. "And I'm calling bullshit on the liver and onion sandwich. No one would do that to a child."

Pulling her shoulders back, Helene said, "There's no need to curse or question me. You didn't know my grandmother. She ate liver as a child and thought it was normal to send that for lunches." When Dr. Austen didn't react, Helene added, "Besides, she didn't want to raise me. She made it clear she was finished parenting."

Dr. Austen nodded. "Now *that's* interesting. Tell me more about that."

14

Helene closed her eyes and felt her jaw tighten again. She'd spent the better part of her adult life trying to forget about her grandmother's distaste for her. She had vowed to leave behind her grandmother's opinion after her wedding day, the last time she was forced to follow her grandmother's wishes.

But Dr. Austen wanted something interesting, and Grammy qualified. Plus, if she could figure out what belief about herself Grammy triggered, maybe Dr. Austen could fix it.

What would it be like if Helene felt comfortable in her own skin? No one understood how draining her daily life was. Putting up a facade of confidence when Grammy had taught her she was unworthy had taken a toll.

That was why she didn't care what other people thought about her. If the person who supposedly loved and cared for you as a child despised you, it didn't matter what anyone else thought.

Exhaling, Helene said, "Fine. Suffice it to say that Grammy didn't expect to be parenting twenty years post-menopause."

She waited for Dr. Austen to comment but only got a nod.

This is ridiculous, she thought, *but the faster I get this over with, the sooner I can get to the baker and see if I can get another week before we have to turn in an order.*

"Grammy and Pappy did the best they could—"

Dr. Austen interrupted, "I would disagree, but go ahead."

Helene interlaced her fingers and put her hands in her lap. "They weren't expecting to have to deal with me. I'd lost my parents and was scared and sad. Nothing was the way it had been. Everything familiar to me disappeared when—"

"Your grandparents were familiar to you. Don't you think you're exaggerating a bit?"

"Do you always interrupt your patients? You'd get more information if you let them finish their thoughts." Helene saw the slight grin on Dr. Austen's face. "Oh. You're trying to get a rise out of me."

The therapist made some notes but didn't say anything else.

"Fine. Whatever. Yes, I knew my grandparents, but I hadn't lived with them before. Spending the night on the weekends wasn't the same as having Grammy help me with homework or pick out my clothes."

The mention of clothes reminded Helene of the prom dress disaster. If Dr. Austen wanted to know exactly what kind of person Grammy was, this story would do it.

"Let me tell you what it was like to have a grandmother dictate how I dressed. Growing up was bad enough, but when I was in high school, Grammy refused to buy me a dress for prom. She said it was a waste of money."

"The dress or prom in general?"

Helene opened her mouth to answer, but nothing came out. She didn't know the answer. Her time in high school was the best and worst time of her life. She'd met Max by then, but she and Grammy hadn't communicated well. If it weren't for Pappy and Max, she would have been completely alone.

"Helene? The dress or prom?"

"I'm not sure, actually. It could have been either." Helene opened and closed the therapy journal before continuing. "I was dating Max by then, and she seemed pleased that he asked me to prom, so I guess it was the dress."

"Did you go to prom, then?"

Nodding, Helene smiled at the memory. "I did. It took some doing. Pappy rallied behind me for weeks. He slipped me money whenever he could. The money he gave me I used for material, since I made the dress myself. Max gave me some money to buy shoes. None of it would have happened, though, if the home economics teacher hadn't taken pity on me too."

"How so?"

The question sent her back thirty-nine years to her fateful trip to the home economics room, 15A.

HELENE STUFFED the polka-dot material for her prom dress into a bag. If Grammy saw the material, she'd ask questions or insult the selection. When she was sure no one would see her, Helene snuck out of the house. She didn't want Grammy to know she had a plan to make her prom dress. Their last fight had ended with Grammy refusing her access to the sewing machine.

"I'm not tying up my precious Singer so you can make a big puffy dress for a silly dance."

"It isn't silly, Grammy. It's my senior prom. The last time I'll be around all my friends," Helene said. That was an exaggeration. The only friend she had was Max, but Helene didn't want Grammy to know that. "I'm making memories for the future. This is going to be my best memory—at least from high school."

Grammy snorted. "Sad if this is the best you can do." Helene didn't know how to respond, but Grammy didn't give her a chance. "Well, do what you want, but keep your hands off my machine."

Helene resorted to using the school's resources. Mrs. Healy, the home economics teacher, encouraged students to use the sewing machines for outside projects. Helene hadn't made it this far to let Grammy stand in her way, so the school machine was her only option.

Thinking no one would be in the room so early, Helene slipped inside. She settled herself into a sewing machine in the front row but jumped when she heard the whirring of another machine. She looked up to find Mrs. Healy bent over one in the back corner of the room. The teacher hadn't noticed her, so Helene waited until the noise stopped before she announced herself.

Mrs. Healy smiled when she saw her.

That's a good sign, Helene thought.

"Hello there! I didn't hear you come in," Mrs. Healy said as she stood up and walked to where Helene had settled. "What are you working on today?"

Helene's face flushed as she pointed at the material. "My prom dress. Here's the material." She pulled a pattern out of her bag. "And an old pattern my grandmother had lying around. I have enough material to make it, I think."

Helene pushed the pattern toward Mrs. Healy. She didn't like it, but she'd spent all the money Pappy gave to her on the material. The pale-blue fabric with white dots was a steal considering how popular it was. The lady at the store said someone had returned it and they couldn't resell it at a regular price. She'd said a silent thank you to Grammy for teaching her to check the clearance rack or she would never have seen the fabric.

Plus, the color would be easy for Max to match when he rented a tux. She'd already gone to the store and found the perfect baby-blue tux she wanted him to get.

Sighing, Mrs. Healy said, "To be young and going to prom. What a magical time in a girl's life." She put down the pattern and began pulling the fabric out of the bag. As she smoothed it out on the table, she said, "This is quality fabric, Helene. It must have cost you a fortune." When Helene explained how she'd gotten the fabric, and Mrs. Healy smiled. "You are so much wiser than your years, dear. I don't think anyone else in my class would have considered buying this. Now, let's see what we can do with it."

In the end, the teacher found another pattern for Helene to use.

"This style suits your body better, and the fabric flows into the full skirt. And look at these ruffles! Who doesn't love polka-dot ruffles?"

When Helene protested that she couldn't pay for the pattern, Mrs. Healy shrugged. "No need. This is a classic. A dress to be worn for years. I'll put it in the school's collection of patterns. No one needs to know who used it first."

As far as Helene knew, no one ever did know who made the dress. She remembered taking Sara on a tour of the high school years later and seeing the pattern in the home ec archives. It amused her that Mrs. Healy and her successors kept it, and Helene laughed out loud. When Sara asked what was so funny, Helene shook her head. "An old memory. That's all."

"WHY DIDN'T you tell Sara how you made your own prom dress?"

Startled by Dr. Austen's question, Helene shook her head. "And let her know how poor and miserable I was growing up? Absolutely not. No child wants to hear their parent relive the past, especially a past as crappy as mine." Helene twisted her wedding ring as she continued. "Are we done for today? I've got errands to run."

Dr. Austen glanced at her watch. "A few more minutes, then you're free to go." With her pen poised over her portfolio, the therapist said, "This story doesn't tell me anything about why your grandmother didn't want to raise you. I could assume she was frugal, protective of her sewing machine, and not the most social person in the world. But there isn't anything concrete that supports your allegation. What story are you telling yourself?"

"What do you mean?" Helene nodded at her therapy journal. "Are you asking what kind of books I read? I don't see how that's relevant to therapy."

Straightening in her seat, Dr. Austen shook her head. "No, nothing like that. How do you see yourself? Are you telling yourself that you're a person worthy of love and kindness, or are you a failure who doesn't deserve to be respected or cared for?" Helene stared back at the therapist, digesting the statements, when she continued. "Everyone falls somewhere in the continuum. What about you?"

A sharp beeping sounded, and Dr. Austen tapped the timer on her phone.

"That's all for today. Same time next week?"

Blinking, Helene nodded as she gathered her things and headed to her car. Of all the things she thought were going to happen today, insight into what she thought about herself wasn't one of them.

15

For the rest of the week, Helene threw herself into wedding plans for Tasha. Dr. Austen would say she was avoiding her assignment, but the questions haunted her.

"What story are you telling yourself? How do you see yourself?"

Helene didn't want to put herself on that continuum because she didn't think she would like the answer. She'd worked so hard to make something of herself. The fear that the real Helene Nevill Shaw wasn't enough drove her crazy.

So, instead of facing it, she retreated and focused on something she could control: Tasha's wedding.

Much to her daughter's dismay.

Helene's breakthrough on manipulating the wedding came when Tasha discovered her gown selection was discontinued. She couldn't help smiling when Tasha called, asking for help.

"I'll go to the Wedding Barn to look at some of the options you found," Tasha had said over the phone, "but, Mom, understand this: I will not be wearing a crown, and we are having donuts at the wedding. Do not pressure me on those."

She'd jumped at the chance to get Tasha a fitting. Luckily,

the bridal store had a cancellation on Friday afternoon. Helene organized it that Greg would pick up Blake from school and take him to soccer practice while Tasha brought Libby to the store to try on dresses.

The only person missing was Sara. Helene envisioned all her family there at the dress shop, like they did on the television show she liked to watch. Logically, she knew Sara was too far away to come for the fittings, but Max pointed out something else to her.

"After everything you and Sara have gone through, do you really think she wants to be in the same room with you?" Max had said. "She moved to another state and told Tasha she doesn't want to be in the wedding if you're involved. Do you understand what that means? Have you talked about this with Dr. Austen yet?"

Helene shrugged off her husband's concerns. She didn't want Max to know she was avoiding the therapist. Instead, she set her sights on the wedding dress selection.

By the time Tasha and Libby arrived at the Wedding Barn, twenty dresses hung in a dressing room for Tasha, and another eight waited for Libby. Darci, the owner, hurried around collecting veils, headpieces, and shoes to complement the selections.

Helene's strategy was simple. She put the gown she wanted her daughter to pick last in line. The designer gown would photograph like a dream for the newspaper's wedding feature. By the time Tasha tried on the other dresses, she would be so relieved there were no more options that she'd pick the last thing she saw.

Making a mental note to confirm with the photographer, Helene saw Tasha's car pull into the parking lot. She hurried over to the table nestled in the corner of the room and grabbed a glass of champagne for Tasha and a cup of sparkling cider for Libby. Helene returned to the middle of the room and stood under the crystal chandelier that adorned the high ceiling of the reception area. Her heels sank into the plush rug, and Helene knew Tasha would be awed at how beautiful the place was.

As her daughter and granddaughter entered, Helene called out, "Welcome to wedding central! Are you as excited as I am?"

Libby glanced up at Tasha. "How do I answer that without hurting her feelings?"

Undeterred by Libby's comment, Helene ignored Darci's coughing fit and rushed forward with the drinks. "You can't hurt my feelings, honey. I'm your grandmother. And this afternoon is going to be one of the most monumental experiences of your life. Trust me."

Libby took the apple cider and sipped it. "Do you have any water?"

Nodding to the table, Helene said, "Help yourself to a bottle. There's popcorn too."

Libby looked around. "Did you bring more cake? It was really good."

"That's too messy for a bridal store. You can't eat food and try on dresses. Can you imagine what Darci would say if you put little chocolate fingerprints on the silk gowns?"

"Popcorn is food." Libby set the cider cup on the table, picked up the water bottle, and headed toward a couch situated in front of a wall covered in diamond shapes. She pulled a book out of her backpack and settled in as if she were going to read. "Why is that allowed?"

"It's a little snack Darci said you could have before we get started. And you have to wash your hands afterward. Sweetie, you need to put the book away. You can't read while you're trying on dresses." Helene turned to Tasha. "Why isn't she excited about this? All girls like frilly clothes."

Tasha wiggled her nose after a sip of champagne. "No, they don't. They might tolerate them, but it's a fact that I do not possess the clothes gene, nor does Libby. We're only here because the dress I picked is unavailable and I don't have the energy or interest to find something else." She finished off the liquid and held out her glass. "More, please."

Helene frowned. "Champagne is for sipping and enjoying. You don't gulp it." She filled the glass half full and handed it back to her daughter. "You need a clear head to evaluate the dresses. And you're driving, might I remind you."

Taking the glass from her mother, Tasha took a sip and put it on the table. "Greg dropped us off and is picking us up. Soccer practice got cancelled. The field flooded after a pipe burst. Greg and Blake went to the arcade and will be here to get us in an hour." The satisfied look on Tasha's face made Helene wonder if her daughter hadn't broken the pipe herself. "Better get a move on."

The shock of a time limit jolted Helene into action. She'd never get Tasha into all those dresses, so she needed another plan. Darci walked into the lobby at that moment and called out, "Is everyone ready to begin?"

"Yes," said Tasha, while Helene and Libby called out, "No," in unison.

Darci shook her head. "I'll come back in a few minutes."

"Wait," Helene said, rushing over to the wedding fitter. "Slight change of plans." Turning back to Tasha, Helene called, "Darci and I are going to get things set up for you. I'll call you back in a minute."

Dragging Darci into the fitting area, Helene put her hand to her chest. If Tasha didn't cooperate soon, she might have a heart attack.

"Mrs. Shaw, you can let go of me now," said Darci. "What is going on?"

Helene dropped the woman's arm and paced. "Tasha's given us one hour to try on dresses."

A frown dulled Darci's face. "That's tight. We can manage

twenty dresses in *two* hours, but you might need to tweak the selections."

"Precisely, which is why we'll select ten out of the twenty dresses we picked. We'll only give her the dresses that have the most potential. And whether she likes it or not, Tasha will choose my favorite dress."

A smile brightened Darci's face. "You are the most manipulative mother of the bride I've ever met. And that's saying something."

"It's for her own good."

Helene wondered what she was going to tell Max about all the dresses she'd purchased to keep Tasha from getting her hands on the one she wanted. It was a twist of fate that Tasha's original dress was discontinued, but it was frantic phone calls and $1,000 to buy the remaining inventory in the tristate area that had gotten her to this point. Darci didn't need that information, though, especially when they were short on time. "We need to get Libby dressed too."

Darci gave her a thumbs-up. "No problem. Let's have both of them come back. I've got dresses ready to go." Darci frowned, and Helene's heart sped up again. "Are you okay if I pare down the selections? We are a bit short on time, and I can reduce the number faster on my own. If that's okay with you."

Under normal circumstances, Helene would have refused the request, but knowing they were short on time, she nodded. "Make sure the dress I chose is the one she selects."

Before she could make Darci promise her, the wedding consultant dashed back to the front of the store. Helene heard Darci chat with Tasha and Libby, giving a rousing pep talk. Helene checked her outfit in the full-length mirrors that surrounded the pedestal in the middle of the fitting area. Satisfied with her appearance, she rejoined the other women. Helene got there in time to see her daughter and granddaughter entering the fitting area.

"Have fun!" Helene said.

Libby frowned. "Aren't you coming back to help, Grandma?"

Hiding her smile, she did an about-face and followed Libby. "Only if you want my help."

∽

Forty-five minutes later, Helene couldn't keep her victory smile off her face. She allowed herself a sip of champagne as she watched Libby twirl around in a ruby-red ball gown with its layers and layers of tulle and the beaded bodice. Her granddaughter refused to try on another dress after slipping into this one. Helene didn't complain, though. This dress coordinated perfectly with her own mother-of-the-bride gown.

Things were going to plan with the wedding dress as well. Tasha appeared mesmerized throughout the session. Her daughter's eyes sparkled as she slipped on one dress after another. Helene made a few comments here and there, but for the most part, she let Darci guide the experience.

And she said she doesn't want a fancy wedding dress.

Relaxing into the sofa, Helene waited for Tasha to come out of the fitting room for the final time. In "the" dress. The dress Helene chose specifically to show off in *The Gazette*. The other dresses were beautiful, but this one was spectacular. It was only a matter of time before Tasha secured the "Wedding of the Year" feature.

The door to the fitting room opened. Libby stopped twirling, and Helene leaned forward in anticipation. This was what she'd been waiting for.

A soft, shimmering, candle-white tulle skirt popped out of the doorway before there was any sign of Tasha. The polka-dotted pattern of crystals and pearls made Helene gasp in pleasure. As her daughter walked into the room, Helene pressed her lips together, keeping her face as neutral as possible.

Tasha's face was anything but. The bride-to-be radiated happiness as she strode into the lobby area, the chapel-length train flowing from the A-line dress. She stepped up on the podium stationed in front of the three-way, full-length mirror. Her eyes were glued to her reflection, and Helene wondered if Tasha even knew she was being watched.

Turning to the right, then the left, Tasha grasped the skirt of the dress in her hands and lifted it out to both sides. The long veil attached to her head blossomed out with the slight breeze the movement made and then settled over her shoulders and arms.

Despite the fact this wasn't the crown she'd requested, Helene surprised herself by not caring. Tasha looked perfect the way she was.

"What do you think?" asked Tasha, spinning around to face her daughter and mother.

"You are beautiful, Mommy!" Libby danced over to her mother and did a funny little bow right in front of her. "You're like the Fairy Godmother in *Cinderella*."

Helene frowned at the mention of the princess.

"You don't like it, Mom?" asked Tasha.

Helene quickly brought her glass to her lips to hide her reaction. Shaking her head, she forced a smile and said, "Don't mind me. I was thinking about something else. You look fabulous in that gown, honey. Darci did an excellent job picking that style for you."

Tasha's eyes studied hers. Helene squirmed at the observation and took another sip of champagne to disguise her discomfort. Finally, Tasha turned back to the mirror and nodded at her reflection.

"This is the one. And I want the veil too."

Darci stepped up beside her. "Can I show you how this gown bustles? You'll need that for dancing and the reception."

Helene remained silent as Darci and Tasha discussed what else needed to be done. They scheduled a time for a second fitting and brainstormed what kind of shoes Tasha should buy. Although this was exactly what she wanted, Helene couldn't rouse herself to contribute to the conversation.

The excitement of the dress selection had disappeared. She didn't know if it was because she got what she wanted or if Libby's comparison had taken the wind out of her sails.

Instead of feeling excited, all Helene wanted to do was go home.

16

Tasha stared at the pictures of her wedding dress on her phone. She still couldn't believe she'd gotten exactly what she promised herself she wouldn't. But it looked so beautiful on her, and it was so comfortable, and Libby liked it, and the wedding coordinator thought it was stunning.

Oddly enough, she didn't think her mother liked it at all. Tasha couldn't get the look of disappointment she saw on her mother's face out of her head. Something was going on with Helene. Twice in one week, her mother had reacted uncharacteristically.

But even her mother's reaction didn't stop her from liking the dress. In fact, she might like it more. So what if she spent more on the dress than she'd intended? Her bank account could stand it. Her lottery win from several years ago meant she didn't need to worry about the occasional extravagant purchase.

"What good is having money if I can't buy myself something nice once in a while?"

Tasha swiped to an image of Libby spinning in her dress.

Despite her objections that she didn't want anything fancy, Libby had been reluctant to change out of the dress. Her daughter had been bitten by the fashion bug.

Even Blake's assessment of his sister hadn't dulled her enthusiasm.

"She looks like a tomato," he'd said when he and Greg arrived to pick them up for dinner.

"She looks beautiful! I can't wait until we can dance at the reception," Greg had said, preventing an argument between the kids. He'd winked at Tasha. "I can't wait to see *your* dress."

"You have to," protested Libby. "Grandma says it's bad luck to see the dress before the wedding."

Helene's lack of response made Tasha uncomfortable. Helene had looked like she was going to be sick. Her face was pale, and she was fidgeting with her wedding ring, something she did when she was nervous. Tasha didn't know for sure, but she thought maybe the therapist had something to do with it. Making a mental note to call her dad later, she closed her photos and headed to the bathroom to get ready for bed.

Before she made it, her cell phone rang. She smiled. Greg was calling to tell her good night, part of their nightly routine. Tasha answered the phone.

"I know I just saw you at dinner, but I miss you already."

"Blech! Look at your caller ID next time," Sara said. "You're too old to be this mushy."

Laughing, Tasha said, "You sound like Blake. Actually, both Blake and Libby. They told us to get a room this afternoon."

"They're too young to understand that, aren't they?"

Nodding to herself, Tasha said, "I think so, but they had a human reproduction chapter in science class. It's about time to have the birds and the bees talk, anyway."

She wasn't looking forward to that, but Greg had offered to sit down with Blake if she wanted help.

"One more reason I'm not having children," said Sara.

"Although, based on my day, you'd think I was working with a bunch of unruly toddlers who don't know how to share."

Tasha flopped down her bed and propped herself up with a pillow. "Rough week?"

"No worse than usual. Still loads better than when I was working with Bill and Rich. I do miss seeing my name up on the shingle. Being part of the Miller Agency is fine but somewhat anonymous."

"You could always go out on your own. There has to be plenty of business in Chicago."

"I like it where I am. Lots to do. Great variety. Good help when I need it."

Tasha's ears perked up. "Oh? Now, what kind of help is Jared offering these days?"

"If you're going to be like that, I'm rescinding my offer to have you come visit next weekend. Send the kids. I don't want to see you."

Knowing it was an empty threat, Tasha said, "Fine by me. You'll have to come here and get them, though. They're too young to fly alone."

"You can send them as unaccompanied minors. I see it all the time when I'm traveling," Sara said. "Although, considering what happened to my luggage last month, I'm not sure I trust the airlines with children."

"True. But you did find out about the Seychelles Islands."

"Which are stunning and someplace I would like to visit someday, but having my clothes end up there when I was in Seattle was a bit of an issue."

"Those islands are gorgeous. Maybe Greg and I should go there on our honeymoon. I'll have to add that to the list. At least I got a dress taken care of today."

"You found somewhere with stock of the one you wanted?" asked Sara. "I thought it was discontinued."

Tasha put her sister on speakerphone and pulled up her

photos again. "It was, which is why I agreed to go to the Wedding Barn with Mom and pick out a dress."

"You didn't!" Tasha winced at the accusation in Sara's voice. "You swore you wouldn't let her hijack this wedding. Do I have to come back and babysit you to make sure you don't end up in that crown as well?"

"Hey, I picked out my own veil. And told Mom she had no choice in the decision. I'm texting you the pictures." Tasha sent the pictures from earlier in the afternoon. "What do you think?"

There was a long pause before Sara spoke. "It's fabulous. You look like a fairy tale princess. I know Mom picked this out, but that is the perfect dress for you."

"So I shouldn't feel bad that Mom helped?"

"You can, but even if she picked out the one she liked, it suits you. I know you wanted something simple, but this will be a showstopper at the ceremony. Libby's dress is cute too. I bet it makes her look like an apple, though—all red and shiny."

"Blake went with tomato. Not sure she'd like the apple comparison either." Tasha paused before she broached the subject. "So, have you given anymore thought to being my maid of honor?"

Sara released a long, slow yoga breath, and Tasha's spirits dropped.

"Never mind. You still have time to change your mind. I don't want to hear you say no yet."

"Hold on, there. Can I answer without having you put words in my mouth?"

A faint hope glimmered in Tasha's chest, and she crossed her fingers. "Sorry. Go ahead. What were you going to say?"

Clearing her throat, Sara said, "I've decided I will come to the wedding. It isn't fair of me to punish you because Mom is a control freak."

Tasha shrieked in happiness, only to cut herself off when she heard Sara continue.

"I do have some conditions, though."

Falling onto the bed, Tasha said, "I can't control her any more than you can. Neither can Dad. This therapist she's seeing seems to have put her into a funk, though. She's been acting strange lately."

"I still can't believe he talked her into that."

Tasha frowned. "It was more of an ultimatum if you ask me. It's been a long time coming." Stretching out, she continued. "What kind of conditions do you have?"

"I need a plus-one for the wedding."

"Well, duh. I knew you and Jared had something brewing. Tell me more."

"It's none of your business." Sara paused, and Tasha wondered why her sister didn't admit what was happening. "My dress has to be flattering."

"Again, duh. But it does have to be red or complement it. Libby loves her dress."

"Can I choose a black dress?" Sara asked. "I've got a great formal for the museum fundraiser and I'd love to wear it again."

"Ever Miss Practical," Tasha teased her sister. "Fine with me. Anything else?"

Sara cleared her throat. "If I have to host a bridal shower or bachelorette party, I don't want to have to invite Mom."

"Not an issue. I don't want either. Anything else, or are we at the point you say, 'Yes, darling sister, I would love to be the maid of honor at your wedding'?"

Sara rewarded her with a hearty laugh. "Fine. If you're going to be so accommodating, I'll be your stinkin' maid of honor!"

Tasha leaned to her bedside table to scribble down Sara's phrase. While she might not want a bachelorette party, that didn't mean she couldn't make silly gifts for her wedding party. She imagined she could find a place to customize a pair of yoga pants. What a great conversation starter for her sister, having to explain why she was a "Stinkin' MOH."

"Thank you! I was worried Mom was going to be the one to stand up and give a toast at the reception for me."

"Which would invariably detail out how your wedding night would be splendid all because she reminded you to do your Kegels three times a day."

The sisters burst out laughing.

"Can you imagine what the minister would say about that?" asked Sara.

"No," said Tasha, "and I have no desire to ever find out."

"Speaking of not finding things out, I don't want you to tell her I agreed to this."

Tasha frowned. "Mom?"

"Yes, Mom. And don't tell Libby either. It wouldn't be fair to her to keep secrets from her grandmother."

"But you want me to lie to Mom?"

"After all the things she's done to you over the years, you're telling me you have a problem with omitting one detail of your wedding?"

"Put like that, no. I suppose I can 'forget' about this for now," said Tasha. "When do you want to pop the news to her?"

Tasha closed her eyes and imagined the evil look of payback on her sister's face.

"I'll let you know when the time is right."

17

Helene called *The Gazette* daily for two weeks after she submitted the application form and pictures for the "Wedding of the Year" feature. She knew irritating the receptionist was a bad idea. Her brief stint answering phones at an architecture firm taught her that. But she couldn't sit back and do nothing. Someone had to know if Tasha would be highlighted.

Helene contemplated who she could call for a favor and it came down to Cybil and Betty. Since Betty still wasn't speaking to her, Helene dialed Cybil's number and waited while the phone rang. The phone went to voicemail.

This is Cybil. I'm teaching a class right now. You know what to do.

She really didn't know what to do, so she left a message asking Cybil to call her back. After she hung up, she looked at the journal sitting next to her cup of coffee on the table. She was beginning to feel like Blake. She hated Wednesdays because that meant a visit to Dr. Austen and a discussion about the blasted stories of her youth.

Helene still didn't understand why this was remotely

important, but when she brought it up with Max, he just shook his head and said, "Eight weeks left. Your choice."

While she didn't believe Max would follow through with his threat of leaving her, Helene didn't want to find out.

She grabbed the coffee cup and filled it before pulling out the kitchen chair and sitting down. Thinking about Cybil teaching class triggered a memory for Helene. She hadn't told the therapist about how she and Max actually met. Grabbing her pen, Helene thought back to her best first day of school ever.

HELENE PICKED AT HER CUTICLES.

"Stop it. That is unladylike. Do you want all these new kids to see how uncivilized you are?" Her grandmother elbowed her as they waited for the principal to get them for their meeting.

Helene hated starting a new school. This would be the tenth one, and she still had two more years of high school to go. She could only hope this was the last school until she escaped to college.

Despite her desire for a stable junior and senior year, she wasn't wild about the town. Glen Valley seemed like such a Podunk place. Sure, it was bigger than some of the other armpits her grandparents had picked to live in, but not by much. The only thing it had going for it was that the high school drew people from several counties. Maybe this would give her an advantage. No one needed to know she lived with her grandparents. Or why.

"Mrs. Parker, Mr. Koster is ready to see you and Helene now." The secretary remained seated and waved them toward the door. "You can go on in."

Helene followed her grandmother but bumped into her when Grammy stopped short at the door. Under her breath, Grammy whispered, "Now, you mind your manners. Don't you dare give this principal any reason to make us move. Do you hear me?"

Nodding, Helene knew now was not the time to remind her grandmother who was really the cause for the moves. That was a discussion she could never win.

The door swung open.

"Mrs. Parker, come in. I'm happy to have you and Helene here today." The principal pumped Grammy's arm up and down before he grasped Helene's hand. "Helene, pleasure to meet you. I do enjoy meeting students for the first time. We don't get a lot of new faces around here."

No need to wonder why, she thought as she glanced around the office. It looked like every other principal's office she'd visited. Trophies and yearbooks stacked neatly on the bookshelf. A clean desk with pictures of what had to be Mr. Koster's family. Her academic file open in the middle of the desk. A boy sitting in the side chair in the far corner of the room.

Hold on. That is different.

She stared at the boy. He looked to be her age, a bit on the scrawny side. His bell-bottom pants seemed fashionable, although the blue plaid bow tie seemed off. But the boy's face stopped her in her tracks.

Shaggy, sandy-brown hair framed his pale, freckled face. Bright-blue eyes stared directly at her, taking her in as she observed him. His perfect lips returned the smile that unexpectedly appeared on her own face.

This was new. Another student meeting her on her first day of school. And a boy at that. Helene ignored boys in general. Grammy insisted on it. But something about this boy was different. Helene's heart beat faster as she wondered why he was here.

"Mrs. Parker, please take a seat. I've invited one of our student ambassadors to escort Helene to her class while you and I talk." Mr. Koster pointed at the boy. "This is Max Shaw.

He's a junior, like you, Helene. He'll get you settled in your classes today."

Helene felt her grandmother tense. Grammy preferred that Helene do everything on her own, including finding her way around a new school. But Helene didn't think her grandmother would put up a stink in the principal's office, especially since the boy was already here.

"Why'd you choose a boy? Didn't you know Helene is a girl?"

A confused look appeared on Mr. Koster and Max's faces. They didn't know Grammy's feelings about men, at least men that came in close contact with her granddaughter.

Mr. Koster cleared his throat. "To be honest, Mrs. Parker, Max was the only ambassador available, and he happens to share several classes with Helene. I assure you, Max is one of our most upstanding students." Then, as if he guessed Grammy's true feelings, he added, "Helene will be in good hands today."

Helene held her breath as she waited for her grandmother's reaction. Would she agree to let her follow this Max around?

I don't care what she thinks. I'd follow him anywhere.

Unsure where those thoughts came from, Helene tore her eyes away from Max and stared at the ground. She didn't want any problems, but she really wanted to spend some time with this boy.

THE PHONE ALARM RANG, jarring her out of her memories. Grabbing the phone, she turned it off. She needed to leave for Dr. Austen's appointment, but she doubted the therapist would find what she had written all that exciting. Plus, she had more important things to do than spend an hour talking about her feelings.

Helene tapped out a quick text to Dr. Austen, cancelling the appointment. She acknowledged she would pay for the session but didn't have time to get there. Helene signed off, saying she would see her next week.

With her morning free, Helene strategized how to improve the chances of Tasha winning the "Wedding of the Year" feature.

18

Max lifted a forkful of mashed potatoes to his mouth. He'd spoken as little as possible since he got home from work. After Dr. Austen called to let him know Helene had blown off her appointment, he'd been too mad to say much.

He was still trying to figure out how to address the issue when Helene asked, "Do you remember how we met?"

Choking down the food, Max gulped some water to collect his thoughts. The headache that had been building since he'd talked with Dr. Austen intensified. "I do. Did that come up in your session with Dr. Austen this week?"

He held his breath. Only eight weeks until Tasha's wedding, and here she was, doing exactly opposite of what he'd asked her to do. It didn't surprise him. She always did what she wanted regardless of what anyone else thought. Max let out his breath in a thin stream. Helene hadn't always been like that.

"I didn't go today."

Max dropped his fork. He looked down at it in surprise. He hadn't thought about letting go of the utensil, but for some reason, it fell from his hand. He made a fist a few times as he thought about Helene's confession. Of all the things he expected, honesty from Helene wasn't one of them. Wondering what had gotten into his wife, he picked up the fork and scooped up some green beans.

"Why is that?"

Dr. Austen recommended open-ended questions. "Let Helene explains things for herself," the therapist had said. "Don't give her a way out of the situation."

Usually, he struggled with this, but tonight it seemed easier to listen than to talk.

Max waited for his wife's response. He watched as she picked the red peppers out of her salad and put them on the side. When they had all been extracted, she arranged them in a straight line. He couldn't stand it any longer.

"What are you doing?" Max asked.

"Eating," Helene said.

"No. With the red peppers. Why are you lining them up?"

Helene looked up at him, blinking as if she didn't understand him.

Frustrated with her lack of response, Max redirected the conversation. "Why didn't you go to Dr. Austen's today? Did you not do the assignment?"

She frowned at him again, but this time he could tell she knew exactly what he asked. Instead of answering, she nodded and stabbed the pile of red peppers with her fork. When she had them on the tines, she glanced back up.

"I did the assignment, which is part of the reason I didn't go."

Frustrated with Helene's obtuseness, Max's vision blurred. Dr. Austen advised against reacting to Helene, but it was tough to keep himself in check. Remembering the therapist's advice, he asserted himself.

"Answer the question, Helene. I can't read your mind." The

words felt harsh coming out of his mouth, but his wife didn't miss a beat.

"Did you know you were the first boy I was ever allowed to interact with? The first boy that Pappy stood behind me on."

He'd expected a flippant response, so he wasn't sure what to do with the one he received. To cover his surprise, he shook his head. He knew Pappy had liked him, but he had no idea the old man had fought for him. "No. You never told me that. Why are you telling me now?"

His vision cleared, and he saw the expression on her face. It reminded him of the Helene he fell in love with. Gone was the schoolmarm expression of determination. Now he saw the timidness and adoration from Helene in her teens.

As much as Max wanted to believe Helene was changing, he couldn't. Throughout the years, he'd seen her pretend to get what she wanted. She might still be doing it today.

The closet full of wedding dresses he'd found was proof. He surmised Helene had bought them to keep Tasha from getting the one she wanted. Never mind that she loved the gown she'd ultimately selected; Max knew Helene had manipulated their daughter into purchasing it. The proof lay in the bridal magazine he'd accidentally knocked off Helene's nightstand. The sticky note labeled *This is it!* in Helene's handwriting, stuck on a page highlighting the dress, said it all. Whatever it was she was doing now may not mean Helene was seeing things from his perspective. She might just be acting like she had been for years.

Her voice pulled him from his thoughts.

". . . and I thought it was time you knew how much you changed my life."

Despite the fact he'd missed the first part of her statement, he couldn't help himself. "Have you ever thought about how much you changed mine?" The shocked expression on her face gave him his answer. "You did. At first, I thought it was good, but lately, I'm beginning to wonder."

He pushed himself back from the table. The sudden movement made his head pound harder, and his stomach protested, threatening to reject the food he'd eaten. Swallowing hard, Max said, "I don't ask a lot of you, but I'm serious about therapy with Dr. Austen. It took thirty-seven years for this situation to evolve. Don't tell me you've figured it all out after two weeks."

"It was three. I did my assignments for the third appointment. I just didn't go."

"Enough." He stood up fast, the room spinning so much he grabbed the edge of the dining room table. "Why can't you take this seriously? It's not a joke."

Desperate to put some space between himself and his wife, Max picked up his plate and stomped out of the room. His feet got heavier as he made it to the kitchen. Scraping the remaining food on his plate into the trash can, Max loaded the plate into the dishwasher. He turned around, the room spinning, and grabbed the counter to steady himself.

The clicking of Helene's heels on the floor pounded like drums, and he struggled to cover his ears. Something touched his shoulder, but when he spun around, he couldn't see what it was. His vision blurred, and his legs gave out from under him. His back and hip connected with the floor, but he didn't feel the pain that should go with the fall.

"Max!" screamed Helene. "What's wrong? Please talk to me. I'm doing the best I can."

He took a deep breath and discovered the air wouldn't fill his lungs. Something was wrong.

19

The rest of the night passed like a nightmare for Helene. She called an ambulance, begging them to hurry. Then she lay down on the floor with Max, stroking his hair and telling him how much she loved him. She didn't know if he could hear her or understand what was happening, but he kept his eyes on hers and squeezed her hand every few minutes.

Once they made it to the hospital, the emergency room staff whisked Max away, leaving her to deal with paperwork and insurance questions. It might have been better that way. At least the paperwork was something she could control. There was nothing else in a hospital that she could.

Helene paced the waiting room, debating whether she should call the girls. Tasha would rush right over, leaving the kids with Greg. Her future son-in-law moved mountains to help Tasha. Even though he wasn't who she'd picked out for Tasha, he was better than what she'd hoped for.

But the chances were that Sara wouldn't answer her call. Her daughter had maintained radio silence since she'd moved, and Helene didn't think a call at eleven thirty on a Wednesday night would go over well. Helene decided not to call either of their daughters until she had something to tell them. She ignored the fact the girls might never forgive her, and she walked out of the waiting room.

Helene found herself in front of a coffee vending machine. While she wasn't thirsty, she needed something to do with her hands. Digging out some spare change, she selected a medium black coffee and shifted from foot to foot while she waited.

She couldn't help comparing tonight to how things went when Grammy had died. That night, they'd fought over what Helene and Max should name their first baby.

"Absolutely not! You will not use the name Doris," Grammy had said. "I don't care if Max likes it and approved. You will not use my daughter's name."

"Grammy, it's my mother's name too. It's to honor her. To keep her in my memory. What's so wrong with that?" Her grandmother's fury confused her. "And it might not be a girl, anyway. If it's a boy, we were thinking Glenn."

"Hush! Why would you name a sweet, innocent child after the Devil?" Grammy massaged her temples. "You've gone and given me a headache. Those names are no good. I gotta get me some aspirin."

Helene followed her grandmother to the tiny bathroom. Along the way, she listened to Grammy's reasons why the two names would be unfit for the baby.

"But why? I don't understand what's wrong with honoring my parents. Lots of people name their babies after relatives."

Grammy sat down on the yellow-and-white-striped toilet lid cover. For the first time, Helene noticed her grandmother's complexion. Her face seemed sallow and even matched the yellowish color of the room. The flicker of concern flew out of her head when Grammy answered.

"It's past time you knew the truth about your parents. Your parents don't deserve honor. Not your momma nor your daddy."

"That's a horrible thing to say. They died young and didn't get to see me grow up."

Her grandmother struggled with the lid of the aspirin bottle. "Damn childproof caps. Stupid invention," said Grammy. She twisted the cap again and then dropped it. "No wonder I have a headache all the time. Can't get the medicine out of the bottle."

Before Grammy could object, Helene bent down and picked it up. She aligned the tabs of the cap and popped it off. "Here." She gave the bottle and the cap to her grandmother. "Now, explain to me why I shouldn't honor my parents."

She watched while Grammy dumped two pills into her hand and shoved the cap back on the bottle.

"Get me a cup of water, will ya?" Grammy asked. "I'm getting dizzy, and I don't want to stand up."

Helene grabbed the cup by the bathroom sink, filled it with water, and gave it to her grandmother. She watched as Grammy tossed the pills into her mouth, then swallowed the water.

After handing the cup back to Helene, Grammy said, "Do you know how your parents died?"

"Of course I do." Helene swallowed hard. She knew her birthday wish hadn't actually killed her parents, but it still made her uncomfortable. "They had a car crash the night of my sixth birthday. They didn't make it to the hospital."

Her grandmother's complexion paled even more than before.

"Oh, they said it was a car crash, but it was your daddy's fault," said Grammy. She put her hand up to her temple and closed her eyes. "The drunk bastard had to go to the bar that night. And, of course, she was too weak to say no. He had no business driving himself around. If that tree hadn't killed him, I would've. He deserved to die for killin' my baby. For running me out of my home." She hoisted herself off the toilet and staggered out the door. "I need a nap."

Helene stood there watching as Grammy toddled down the hallway and pushed open her bedroom door. Something told her she should follow her grandmother and make sure she was okay, but her feet froze to the floor.

What did Grammy mean, her daddy killed her mother? Both of her parents had died instantly in the car accident, hadn't they? Was this just Grammy being cantankerous? The woman who couldn't be happy and refused to let anyone around her be joyful. The woman who went out of her way to tell her granddaughter what a loser she was. The woman who should have been looking out for her from the start.

But if what her grandmother said was true, then it made perfect sense. Grammy really didn't want her because she would be a reminder of what had happened to her own daughter.

Helene pushed herself off the bathroom wall and shuffled back to the living room. In the fog of processing Grammy's words, she bumped into Pappy as he was coming in the front door.

Grabbing hold of her arm, Pappy said, "Hey there, sweetie. What's got you so preoccupied?" He nodded to her belly. "Is the baby worryin' ya?"

She blinked. Pappy would know the truth. He could clear this up. Shaking, she wrapped her arms around herself as she struggled to put her thoughts together.

"You look like you seen a ghost," said Pappy. He took her arm and pulled her into the living room. Guiding her to a chair, he motioned for her to sit before he asked, "What's wrong?"

Remaining on her feet, Helene stood up straight. As much as she didn't want to, she needed to know. She wasn't sure why, but she felt it in her gut. Blinking back tears, she looked up at Pappy. "Is it true? Did my father kill my mother?"

The blood drained from Pappy's face, and she knew. Her father was a monster, and her mother was a pushover. Her shaking got worse as Helene waited for Pappy to speak.

"She finally told you, huh?"

The realization she'd been lied to for years unraveled something inside her. The people she'd spent her life with, the two people she loved and trusted, had never been completely honest with her.

"Why didn't you tell me?"

"She didn't want ya to know." Pappy shrank in front of her. He wobbled to his beat-up recliner and slumped into the chair. "She never forgave Doris for gettin' pregnant with you. That's why she's so hard on ya. She didn't want ya to end up like your momma." He took off his ball cap, his wispy, thinning hair poking out at all angles. "She wanted to protect you. Like she couldn't your momma. The drinkin' didn't start until after you was born. But by then, it was too late."

Not knowing what to make of her grandmother's behavior, Helene asked, "Is that why we moved? Because of the accident?"

Pappy nodded. "People talk. Blamed yer grammy and me for not steppin' in sooner. She never got over that."

Helene let out an unsteady breath. "So she took it out on me all these years. To punish me." Overwhelmed by the situation, she flopped onto the couch. "She didn't need to, though. I blamed myself. It was my fault."

"Why would you think that?"

Helene lowered her head, ashamed by what she was going to admit. "I made a wish on my birthday. I wished that Daddy wouldn't drink anymore and I could live someplace different." She looked through her tears at Pappy. "I got my wish."

"It wasn't your fault, sweetie. Your daddy loved you and

Doris. He had a problem he couldn't handle, and it caused an accident. That's all."

Cold seeped into her body as she'd never felt before. Pappy could say whatever he wanted, but now she knew the truth.

Staring Pappy in the eyes, she said, "Do you know what I remember most about my father? The smell of bourbon. I thought it was just the way daddies smelled... until Max came home one night after meeting some friends at the bar. That's when I figured out the smell of bourbon doesn't mean love. It just means you're drunk.

"I was six, and I knew Daddy drank too much. I even bought into the lie that it was a rainy night and the roads were slick. No. It was because he was a drunk, and he didn't care who he hurt. At least my mother died. Look what happened to me."

Pappy waved his hands in the air. "What's that supposed to mean? You're all grown up, married, and about to have a baby on your own. You did okay."

"My life is a lie. Because of you and Grammy, it's not what I thought it was." Helene patted her pregnant belly. "Grammy was right. My father killed my mother. That's the story I have to tell my child." Pushing herself off the couch, Helene walked to the door. "I can't be here anymore. I'll call you later."

She didn't know it when she left, but that was the last time she'd see Grammy or Pappy alive. Helene ignored Pappy's phone calls until it was too late. A few days later, the hospital called, letting her know that both Grammy and Pappy were gone. Grammy's headaches predicted the stroke that took her life, and Pappy died of a broken heart, grieving the only woman he'd ever loved.

And leaving Helene more alone and guilt-ridden than ever before.

. . .

"Excuse me." A voice startled Helene, reminding her she was still standing in front of the vending machine. "Your coffee is ready."

Nodding, she took the cup and headed back to the waiting room. It was time to call Sara and Tasha.

20

Helene pulled her gaze off the waiting room television to watch her daughter. Tasha sat in the corner, murmuring into her cell phone. She'd arrived shortly after 8:00 a.m., much to Helene's relief. Tasha had offered to come as soon as Helene called the night before, but she'd convinced her daughter to wait until the kids went to school.

"It will be less traumatic for them, dear."

"Greg said he could stay with the kids." Helene heard the hitch in her daughter's voice. "I want to see Dad in case he—"

Helene had cut her daughter off. "You can see him in the morning. He is stable. The doctors ruled out a stroke and a heart attack, so whatever we're dealing with has to wait until morning. They aren't running anymore tests tonight."

Now Helene wished Tasha had come sooner. It was lonely sitting in the hospital all night. She had nodded off a few times, but the chairs in the waiting room were uncomfortable, and she was too worried about Max to relax. Helene put on a brave face for her daughter, but inside, she was terrified.

"Sara can't make it until tomorrow." Helene moved over as

Tasha tucked the phone into her pocket and sat down next to her on the couch. "She has a court appearance today, and, since Dad's stable, she decided to wrap that up then leave first thing in the morning. I'll get her flight info when I call her with the doctor's update."

Nodding, Helene stared at the television that was broadcasting a popular game show. She watched as the contestants struggled to answer obscure trivia questions. This was something she could do. Random trivia may not help her communicate with her family, but it took her mind off what was happening around her.

"The Louvre," she said when the host asked for the name of the most popular museum in the world. "Everyone knows that."

"You'd be surprised," said Brad Gerome as he walked into the waiting room, his partner, Carlton Reynolds, close behind.

Getting to her feet, Helene relaxed into Brad's embrace. She'd hoped Brad and Carlton would stop by, but she didn't feel like she could call them herself. It was always nice to have the men around. They tended to be more sympathetic than her daughters or husband.

Helene shuddered. Her husband might be dying, and she was complaining he wasn't supportive enough.

"You didn't have to come," she mumbled into his shoulder. "How did you find out?"

"Tasha called," said Carlton as he joined Brad in giving her a hug. "We wanted to be here for you. Do you have any more news?"

Shaking her head, she caught Tasha's eye and mouthed, "Thank you." Her daughter winked back. Even though Brad wasn't officially Tasha's brother-in-law anymore, Helene still liked it when he was included in family things.

"The last report was that he was stable. But they are waiting for some test results. We could be waiting all day."

"Have you had anything to eat?" Carlton slid a small cooler off his shoulder before he continued. "I grabbed a few things for you just in case. Little snacks to keep you going until you know how long you'll be here. Hospital food is okay, but you might like something homemade."

Tears came to her eyes, and she looked away to get a hold of herself. "Thank you. We were cleaning up dinner when Max ... ," Helene swallowed to keep the emotion from overcoming her, "when he collapsed." Striving to keep calm, she nodded at Tasha. "Tasha talked to Sara. She'll be here tomorrow." Helene pointed up at the television. "All I'm capable of right now is answering quiz questions. I'd have $15,000 if I were a contestant today."

Carlton guided her down onto the sofa, keeping his arm around her shoulders. "This has been a shock. It's okay to think of something else for a while."

Helene let Carlton console her. She wouldn't remember the exact words he said later, but it felt good to mentally check out after everything that had happened. She peeked over at Tasha and Brad. They sat together on the other side of the waiting room, quietly talking about something.

She knew she was overreacting, but Helene couldn't help wondering if they were blaming her for what happened. They weren't wrong. Tasha had every right to be mad at her. This would change her trip to Chicago with the kids. It might delay the wedding.

She was a terrible person. What kind of wife argued with her husband so much he ended up in the hospital? And to argue over going to a therapist after she'd already promised to change was proof she was self-centered and didn't deserve what she had.

Carlton's voice broke into her thoughts. "Do you want to talk about what happened?"

Helene froze. Now was the perfect time to confess what

she'd done, but she didn't think she was ready for the disappointment and blame that came with a confession. She needed more time.

Max was right. She should be going to her weekly sessions with Dr. Austen. If she had, Max wouldn't be in the hospital, and she wouldn't be spinning out of control, wondering if she was the reason bad things happened to her family.

"Helene?" Carlton asked. "Are you okay?"

She nodded and gave Carlton a weak smile. "Just tired. That's all."

With that, she turned back to the television in time to answer the question about which river ran through Paris.

∼

Four game shows and several hours later, Brad and Carlton left after the doctor updated them on Max's condition.

"He's stable and responsive. We ruled out a stroke and a heart attack. No arrhythmias either." The doctor frowned. "Usually, I find something that caused a reaction like this. His blood pressure meds need to be adjusted, but otherwise, Mr. Shaw seems fine. I'll run a few more tests and monitor your husband while I wait for his cardiologist to get back to me."

Despite the fact that this was her opportunity to confess to her part in Max's situation, Helene nodded and thanked the doctor before she shooed Tasha from the hospital.

"Go home. Get some rest. You should be there when Libby and Blake get home from school. If you aren't, they're going to worry." Helene appealed to her daughter. "You can't do anything here at the moment. Plus, I need you at your best when Sara comes." She gave Tasha what she hoped was a rueful smile. "We'll need a referee since your dad isn't up to keeping me in check."

Stretching her arms over her head, Tasha nodded. "As

much as I don't want to admit it, you're right." She hugged Helene before she gathered up her purse. "Sara's coming to my house from the airport. I'll call you to see where Dad is before we head this way. Let me know if anything changes. Promise me?"

Helene nodded, then watched Tasha leave the waiting room before she let herself fall onto the couch. She noticed how wrinkled her pants were and, for the first time since Max had collapsed, she wondered what her hair and face looked like.

"Nothing like a medical emergency to make me forget my vanity," she mumbled to herself.

She forced her face to relax, realizing she hadn't made one comment to Tasha about frown lines or wrinkles. Max would appreciate that as well.

Tears pricked at her eyes when she thought about her husband lying in an ICU bed, all alone.

This was her fault, regardless of whether the doctor thought Max's blood pressure played a role. The stress and anxiety of putting up with her had finally taken its toll on her husband. She never should have skipped her appointment with Dr. Austen, nor should she have spent so much time interfering with Tasha's wedding.

A thought caused Helene to sit up a little straighter. Had Max found out about the dresses in the guest closet? He didn't usually snoop around, but he had seemed more irritated than usual when they sat down for dinner. Maybe she should get rid of them, on the off chance Sara or Tasha came to the house to help with Max's recovery.

Slow down, Helene thought to herself. *We don't even know what's happening to Max, let alone when he'll be out of the hospital.*

Guilt washed over her as she recognized she was doing it again. Instead of focusing on her ailing husband and fessing up to her actions, she was covering them up.

If she was going to confess that she had caused Max's hospitalization, she needed to know for sure that was what had happened. That was more important than confessing to causing Grammy's stroke all those years ago. And more important than that was being sure she was a supportive mother to her daughters before it was too late.

Helene grabbed her purse and rummaged around for her phone. She needed to talk to Dr. Austen. Now.

21

Helene fluffed the pillows behind Max. She'd brought some from home because the ones at the hospital didn't seem firm enough to her.

"You don't have to do that, Helene." Her husband's voice sounded tired and old. It had been that way since he woke up in the hospital. "The doctor said it would be good for me to get out of bed and walk around."

Shushing him, Helene turned to adjust the flowers on the bedside table. "The doctor also said you need to take things easy for a few days. You just had an unexplained episode two days ago. One more day with me and the nurses taking care of you is okay." Ignoring her worry, she checked her to-do list. "The cardiologist is supposed to be here between three and four, so what about a sponge bath before then?"

Helene noticed the weariness in Max's eyes, but before he could say anything, Betty piped up from the door, "As much as I love you both, I don't want to see that." She walked into the room with a huge basket full of baked goods. "I brought refreshments!"

Helene hesitated. Her last conversation with Betty had been

anything but amicable, so this visit must be for Max's benefit only. She stepped aside to let Betty approach his bedside but was surprised when Betty pulled her into a big hug. Helene hugged her back and smiled when she heard Betty whisper in her ear.

"You've got a lot on your plate right now. I know what I said last week, but if you need anything, call me."

Dabbing her eyes with her sleeve, Helene busied herself with the basket as Betty fawned over Max.

"So, what's this about you being sick?" said Betty, never one to sugarcoat things. "Roger Gerome's telling everyone at the coffee bar about your 'medical event.'" She used air quotes around the words *medical event*. "He said it's a way for you to get out of the upcoming bowling tournament. He thinks you're scared to lose."

"No way!" Max laughed with more energy than Helene had heard since he'd been admitted to the hospital. "In fact, I'm asking the cardiologist this afternoon about the tourney. I've got two weeks to get back on my feet."

"Absolutely not!" said Helene before her husband could continue. "Your health is more important than a bowling tournament."

Max opened his mouth to speak, but Betty interrupted.

"You might consider listening to her on this one. Greg volunteered to take your place. He's a ringer from what I understand." Betty winked at Helene. "And Tasha would never forgive you if you couldn't walk her down the aisle this time. She's not planning on a third wedding, so this is your last shot."

"Not my fault she couldn't wait for me last time," Max grumbled, but his grin belied his feelings. "So, Betty, tell me what's been going on in the real world. I'm getting tired of hearing about the benefits of an MRI over a CT scan and what type of dye is used in an angiogram."

"Glad you asked. Scoot on over, and I'll get you up to

speed," Betty said, hauling herself onto the edge of the bed. She waved at Helene. "This may take some time. Why don't you take a walk around the new reflection pond Brad built? There's some nice shade and comfy chairs in the ramada. I've got an hour or so before I have to be back at the Coffee Bar. We'll be fine."

Standing at the end of the bed, Helene recognized a dismissal when she heard one. She grabbed her purse and headed out of the room. Hospital smells irritated her nose, so she welcomed the chance to enjoy some fresh air. Between the nurses and Betty, Max was in good hands. It felt right to give him some space. He didn't seem to want her around, anyway.

Helene walked to the elevator and punched the down button. While she waited, she thought about what the doctor had told her earlier that morning.

"Other than his blood pressure, there is nothing physically wrong with your husband. I got the impression from him that things are tense at home." He had held up his hand when Helene protested. "None of my business. But you need to know that anxiety and stress can trigger events like the one Mr. Shaw had on Wednesday night. Whatever the issue, it needs to be resolved so your husband can heal."

"You can't give him a prescription or anything?"

The doctor shook his head. "He doesn't need another one. Once we get his blood pressure under control, he needs to rest and recover stress-free."

The elevator arrived, and Helene waited for several people to get off before she entered and pressed the button for the lobby. She leaned back against the cold metal wall, enjoying the chill on her back. Helene closed her eyes and willed the tension in her neck and back to release. As much as she didn't want to admit it, Betty was right. She needed to get away for a few minutes, if for no other reason than to decide what to do next.

Helene followed the signs from the elevator to the reflection pond. Blooming plants and shrubs surrounded the newly built ramada. She didn't know what they were, but the yellows, pinks, and purples soothed her. The newspaper's photos of the area hadn't done justice to Brad's design. What looked like a simple shade structure was an intricate mixing of materials. Native rock and stone outlined the reclaimed wood from the old hospital fence, making the wood the focal point for the only wall of the structure. She needed to add a note to her to-do list to call *The Gazette* and demand they come back for better pictures.

She continued to the ramada and lowered herself into one of the cushioned chairs. Her joints protested after sitting in the stiff visitor chair in Max's hospital room. Even the cot the hospital let her sleep in wasn't as comfortable as this chair. Letting out a sigh, Helene replayed her conversation with Dr. Austen. The therapist had returned her call earlier that morning before the sun was even up.

"I don't normally answer calls like this, but my day is booked solid, and you sounded upset," Dr. Austen said. "You wouldn't call if it weren't an emergency, would you?"

"It's all my fault," Helene cried. "Everything. The hospital, the stroke. If I could figure out what's wrong with me, no one would have died."

"Hold on," the therapist had said. "Slow down and tell me what's going on. Where are you?"

It took a few minutes to catch Dr. Austen up with what happened to Max and her part in her grandmother's death, and even then, Dr. Austen didn't seem convinced.

"Helene, from what you just told me, you are not responsible for Max's illness, no more than you are for your grandmother's death."

"But I'm the last one either of them talked to before it happened. They were both frustrated with me and argued with me right before they got sick." Helene almost added, "And died," but she wouldn't let herself think that way about Max. "I'm the common factor here. The doctor said stress might have done this."

"Emphasis on 'might.' You do have to consider high blood pressure, a cholesterol problem, and a lifetime of eating unhealthy foods, at least for your grandmother," said Dr. Austen. "Helene, you're a pain in the ass, no doubt, but you cannot blame yourself for things you didn't do."

Even the revelation of how Helene's parents had died didn't sway the therapist.

"Your father had a drinking problem. He made the decision to drink and drive. It was your mother's decision to get into the car with him. You were a child who made a birthday wish. Don't blame yourself for something you had no control over."

Helene cried before Dr. Austen interrupted her with a new assignment. Before Helene's next appointment, she needed to write an apology letter to herself.

"I don't need to see it, but I'll know if you wrote it."

"How? Do you have ESP or something?" Helene joked through her tears.

"It's easy to tell when a patient has given themselves grace. Test me if you want, but if you do this for yourself, you'll feel better. Trust me on this."

SHE DID BELIEVE DR. AUSTEN, and she would write the letter. But the comfortable chair and beautiful surroundings begged for a nap. And before she knew it, Helene had closed her eyes and dozed off.

22

Rolling her carry-on through the hospital, Sara followed Tasha's directions to their father's room. Usually, she would leave her suitcase in her rental car, but there was no rental. The company had cancelled her reservation by mistake. Thankfully, there was a taxi available, or she would have had to call her sister or, God forbid, her mother to come pick her up.

But as the bag hit her leg again, she regretted not going to Tasha's house first. Another hour wasn't going to change anything. She should have stopped by, dropped off her bags, hugged her niece and nephew, and grabbed something to eat before plunging herself into an unknown situation with her parents. To prove the point, her stomach growled.

"Yeah, got it," she said to herself at the same time she saw the door to her father's room. Taking a deep breath, Sara steeled herself for whatever she was about to find. She approached the door and heard laughter coming from inside.

Not expecting that, she paused and continued listening. She recognized her father's voice but couldn't place the female one. She relaxed a bit, then felt guilty. It wasn't fair of her to be happy she didn't have to deal with her mother right away, but it was her natural reaction.

Opening the door, Sara peeked in. She watched as Betty continued whatever story she was telling her father, using her arms to indicate some grand event that was probably an exaggeration. Before Betty finished the story, Max called out, "Sara, quit lurking in the doorway and give your old man a hug."

The tears that sprang from her eyes surprised her as she rushed to her father's bed. She valued her independence and pragmatism, but the sight of her father lying in a hospital bed broke her resolve.

"Daddy!" she muttered as she dropped her bags before leaning down to hug him. She buried her face in his shoulder and, by the time she pulled away, Max's hospital gown was wet with her tears. "Sorry. I didn't plan to react like that." She turned to Betty. "I didn't expect to see you here." She leaned in for a hug, but the intensity of Betty's embrace surprised her. Sara squeezed the woman back, then pulled away. "Who's manning the Coffee Bar for you?"

"I've got a part-timer who's reasonably efficient. It's nice to see you. We've missed you. Renee's missed you the most. Office isn't the same without you." She glanced at Max, then down at her watch. "I'd better head back now. No sense testing my luck, especially right now. The riverfront renovations jumpstarted my lunchtime business." Betty patted Max's foot before she walked to the door. "You listen to the doctors, you hear?"

Sara waved at Betty and waited until the door closed before she turned back to her father.

"How are you feeling? Tasha's been updating me, but do you have anything new to report? I'm sorry I didn't get here sooner, but work has been crazy. Jared wanted to come with me, but I told him I'd rather make the trip myself."

The smile on her father's face stopped her.

"What? Why are you looking at me like that?"

"Seems strange—your boss offering to join you at a family emergency." He winked at her. "You and Jared an item now?"

Sara considered denying it. Instead, she shrugged. "Yeah. We are. I should have told you, but—"

"You don't need to apologize. You're entitled to your own life. I understand that." He patted the bed, and Sara sat down beside him. "I'm doing pretty well. The doctors aren't sure what it was, but they expect a full recovery." He cleared his throat before continuing. "I'm not sure I can say the same for your mother, though."

Sara shifted so she could see her dad's face. "Why's that?"

"She's blaming herself for whatever happened."

Sara bit her tongue to keep from agreeing with her mother. While she knew it wasn't true, dealing with Helene's self-centeredness and narcissism couldn't be good for her father. Instead of venting her frustration, Sara looked around the room. "Where is she?"

"Down at the reflection pond. Betty told her to get some air." Max frowned. "She's been down there quite a while, though. I wonder what's she's doing."

"She probably ran into someone from Bunco or the club and lost track of time while she was talking." Sara's shoulders tensed as she thought of her mother promoting her own social status when she should be helping her husband. Instead of getting herself worked up about her mother, she asked, "Is there anything I can do right now? Are you hungry?"

She followed Max's finger and saw the huge basket of treats from Betty's store.

"If you want something, help yourself. There's got to be something in there you like."

Sara started to pass on the offer, but her stomach took that opportunity to make its presence known again.

"Okay, that sounds good." Sara dug through the basket as she continued peppering her father with questions. By the time she found her preferred oat bran muffin, she felt caught up with his medical issues. "So, when do you think you'll go home?"

"Insurance wants me out sooner than later, so I'd guess tomorrow, Sunday at the latest. How long are you staying?"

Sara swallowed a bite of muffin before replying, "I've told Jared a week, but I can swing two weeks if you need me. It depends on how long Tasha and I can stand to live under the same roof."

Max stared at the muffin his daughter was eating and said, "Why don't you get a hotel room? It's not that far of a drive."

"Tasha asked me to stay at the house, and in a moment of weakness, I acquiesced. She and the kids had planned to come to Chicago this weekend, but I'm here instead. It'll be fun to hang out with Libby and Blake. Promises of pizza and shopping have been made." She checked her watch again. "Shouldn't Mom be back by now?"

Her father grinned. "Are you trying to leave before she sees you?"

Sara cringed. "Am I that transparent?"

"No," said Max, shaking his head. "It's understandable, though. She hasn't been the easiest person to deal with lately." He started to say more, but the door opened, and a nurse strode in.

"Good afternoon, Mr. Shaw. Time to check your vitals." The nurse nodded at Sara before logging into the computer station in the corner of the room. "Your visitor might want to wait outside while we go through things."

Sara started to collect her things when Max said, "This is my daughter. She's welcome to stay if she wants."

"That's okay, Dad." She hefted her briefcase to her shoulder. "I told Tasha I'd be there before the kids got home from school. If I leave now, I should make it. I'll come back tomorrow."

"Don't you want to say hello to your mother?" The serious

tone of Max's voice made Sara wonder if she would offend her father with a truthful answer, but a quick glance at his face told her he already knew. "That's okay. I don't think she's ready to see you either."

Sara leaned down to hug her father. So the nurse couldn't hear, she said, "Thank you for understanding. I promise I'll see her before I go."

With that, Sara hurried out of the room.

23

The next few days passed quickly. While she was relieved Max was out of the hospital, the house was filled with nonstop visitors. Helene normally enjoyed social calls, but after serving refreshments to seven bowling teams, twelve coworkers, and a gaggle of high school chums, Helene lost her patience. She banned visitors for the rest of the week. Her ban, however, did not go without complaints.

"Collette thinks you're a mean old woman," said Max when she brought in his Tuesday afternoon snack. "Care to defend yourself?"

Helene remembered the captain of the Gutter Girls' complaint as she and the rest of her bowling team had been kicked out of the house the previous day. "You're a stick in the mud. Max needs our support more than ever. Especially since all he has is you."

Rather than share Collette's sentiments with Max, she put his tray on his lap and said, "Here you are. A little something before dinnertime."

Max's eyes narrowed. "Why do I have to eat blueberries again?" he asked, nodding at the bowl of fruit on his tray. "I don't particularly like them. And what is this grainy stuff you sprinkled on top of it? It tastes like sawdust."

Pushing her hair out of her face, Helene put a clean set of pajamas on the foot of the bed. "It's flaxseed, dear. Your new diet calls for a daily serving of it and the berries. The website I'm following recommended combining both for efficiency."

"Clearly not for taste," said Max. He grimaced as he chewed another spoonful of the mixture. "I'd rather risk another trip to the hospital than eat this."

Helene jerked at the comment and knocked the bottoms off the bed. Bending down to pick them up, she said, "Bite your tongue. What a horrible thing to say."

While she watched her husband eat his snack, Helene wallowed in guilt. The doctor was right. Max needed a stress-free life, and it was her fault he was disturbed. All the self-denial she'd been employing throughout the years did nothing to her, but it hurt the person she loved most. Now she'd made it worse by compounding her part in Max's condition with her guilt about her grandmother's death. She forced herself to put that on hold until she saw Dr. Austen.

As fast as she could, she refolded the pajamas and replaced them.

"I'm going to the kitchen for some tea. Do you want anything?"

"How about a glass of red wine? That's on my diet, right?" Panic flared in her chest at her husband's suggestion, but Max winked at her. "I'm only joking. Tea would be fine."

Before he could tease her again, Helene hurried out of the room. She made it to the kitchen, filled the tea kettle with water, and put it on the stove to boil. Plopping down in the chair, she allowed herself to close her eyes.

The image of all the people coming in and out of the house filled her mind. She couldn't shake the feeling that the constant flow of visitors had been like a viewing at a funeral home. Everyone coming by to gawk at the dead guy.

Helene shook her head and muttered to herself, "Overreacting a bit, don't you think?"

Instead of dwelling on the negative, she turned to other pressing matters, like who was going to stay with Max tomorrow when she went to her appointment with Dr. Austen. Helene considered her options. Tasha had a PTO meeting. Brad and Carlton both had to work, and Greg was out of town. That's when Helene remembered Betty's offer from the hospital. She grabbed her phone and called her for help.

"Can you come sit with Max tomorrow, please? I've got an appointment at eleven, and I don't want to leave him here alone. Everyone else I've asked is busy."

"Sorry. No can do. The part-timer I hired gave Ida May the wrong lunch."

Helene didn't understand. "Why is that a problem?"

"Because Ida ended up with Eveline Gerome's order, and all hell broke loose. Now Eveline thinks she's gonna get a free lunch from me to fix the mistake. I need to be there to stop that in its tracks. What about Sara? Why can't she sit with her dad?"

Helene pondered Betty's question. Mother and daughter had avoided each other since Sara's arrival at the hospital. Sara called Max twice a day and stopped in at least once, but somehow Max managed to keep them separate. She wondered if she should be offended by her husband and her daughter's collusion, but knew it was for the best.

She couldn't avoid Sara forever. Her daughter was the perfect person to be here while she was gone. And she'd left it for too late in the day to find anyone else.

She tapped out a text message of what she hoped was an acceptable request. *Can you stay with Dad tomorrow from 10:30 to 1? I have an appointment. It's too soon to leave him alone, and Tasha is busy.*

Her finger hovered over the send key. If he weren't in bed recovering, Helene would have asked Max to read her text. She wanted it to sound polite and not demanding. Her daughter hated it when she felt like she was being pressured to do something. Releasing the breath she was holding, she tapped send, then went to the stove to see if the water was boiling yet.

As she glanced at the tea kettle, she muttered under her breath, "A watched pot never boils. One thing Grammy was right about."

Helene's phone signaled an incoming text. Wiping her moist hands on her wrinkled slacks, she picked up to see Sara's response.

Yes. Tell Dad I'll see him at 10:45.

She held the phone in her hand, rereading her daughter's response. Succinct. To the point. Not emotional. One could argue that Sara was being cold. Not that Helene didn't deserve it. Nothing between them was easy, and maybe she made it worse. But Max needed a peaceful environment, and it didn't make sense for anyone to get upset about something as simple as who was staying with whom.

The tea kettle whistled, interrupting Helene's spiraling thoughts. She rushed to the stove top and put together a tray to take to Max. First tea with her husband. Then write a letter of apology to herself. As she carried the tray to Max's room, Helene couldn't help but pine for the feeling of grace that Dr. Austen promised would come with forgiveness.

24

The next day, Helene left the house for her appointment before Sara arrived. She was grateful she'd agreed to stay with her father while she was gone, but Max agreed with her. A conversation with Sara before therapy would upset her too much to have a productive session with Dr. Austen. Helene didn't bother to tell Max how much she needed this session. The acknowledgment of killing Grammy weighed on her, and she needed to process the guilt with someone.

Dr. Austen's waiting room was empty when Helene let herself in, and the interior door to the doctor's office was open. Relieved that she wouldn't be running into Eveline today, she poked her head into the therapist's office. Dr. Austen sat in her chair, gazing out the window.

"Good morning," Helene said. "Are you ready for me?"

The therapist swiveled around and waved her in. "I am. Please take a seat. How is Max doing?"

Making her way to the couch, Helene settled herself in her seat before answering. "Good. He's feeling better, and all his tests have come back normal. Provided he follows doctor's orders, it shouldn't happen again."

"That's good to hear. I miss having him come in for our sessions. Any idea when he will be back?"

"The follow-up appointment with the doctor is in two weeks. We should know then."

Dr. Austen grabbed her ill-monogrammed portfolio and scribbled some notes before continuing. "So. Let's talk about what happened the night Max had his incident. He sounded fine to me when I talked to him on the phone that day. Worried you didn't show up for your appointment, but I never suspected he'd end up hospitalized."

The guilt Helene had kept at bay for the last week washed over her, and she struggled to keep her shoulders squared and back. Determined to be honest with herself and the therapist, Helene said, "We were arguing. Max got fed up with me and walked to the kitchen, where he collapsed. The stress of living with me for this long finally got to him, and his blood pressure skyrocketed. I'm the reason he's sick." She brushed away a tear as she prepared herself to deliver the next bombshell. "Just like I killed my grandmother."

Dr. Austen's pen tapped against the portfolio. "Helene, we went over this," the therapist said. "You didn't kill your grandmother."

"Then why do I feel like it's my fault?" She stood up as she explained what had happened again. Maybe the doctor hadn't understood her on the phone. "We were arguing about what to name Sara. I wanted to name the baby after my mom or dad, and that's when she told me about how my father killed my mother. I was furious and walked out on her. But I never got to apologize before she died."

Dr. Austen shook her head. "The shock of learning the truth about your parents made you angry." She reached for a box of tissue and handed it to Helene. "The two of you argued, which affected your grandmother. You blame yourself for her death. I understand that. But you didn't *kill* her."

Using a tissue, Helene dabbed at her eyes, taking care not to smudge her waterproof mascara. How gauche would that be?

Helene cleared her throat. "Fine. The stroke killed her. I didn't make it happen, but I contributed to it. I was the biggest contributing factor. Just like I was with Max and his incident."

Dr. Austen leaned back in her chair and steepled her fingers together. "Helene, Max's blood pressure skyrocketed, and the doctor said his medicine wasn't working. You can't blame yourself for that."

She crumpled up the wet tissue and grabbed another. "I could have made him go to the doctor." Her head jerked up. "Wait a minute. How do you know about his blood pressure? I didn't tell you that."

"No, Max did. He made an appointment for a physical too. I encouraged him to start taking control of more things so you didn't have to."

"Why would you do that? I'm perfectly capable of making his appointments."

"And he's an adult male who shouldn't rely on you to do things he can do on his own." Dr. Austen cocked her head to one side. "Tell me, Helene, do you like being in control?"

"Of course. Doesn't everyone?"

"No, as a matter of fact, they don't. Some people want someone else to take control of things so they don't have to worry about the details. Or so they don't have to take responsibility for the things that happen.

"For example, I work with husbands who never plan a vacation. They let their wives make all the arrangements, they go on the trip, and they complain the entire time because they didn't get to do the things they wanted to do."

Helene said, "Then they should have helped plan it."

Dr. Austen gave a slight nod and continued. "What if the wife doesn't want help?"

Helene opened her mouth to respond, but the words died on her lips. Dr. Austen's description was strangely familiar. For as long as she could remember, she did things as she wanted them done. She organized the parties and vacations. Max didn't argue with it, but as she sat on Dr. Austen's couch, she acknowledged that Max didn't contribute either. Helene struggled to wrap her head around what she thought Dr. Austen was saying.

"Hear me out. Your grandmother's death changed you. More so than your parents' deaths. Don't misunderstand me. Losing your parents at a young age shaped you. But when I listen to Max, he tells a story about a young woman who was open and loving, who was shy and sensitive. Max still sees you like this—or he wants to—but you already know that, or you wouldn't be sitting in front of me."

Helene held back a sob. She'd been so long focused on herself that she didn't see how much this had affected Max until now.

"Helene, you changed when your grandmother died. She dumped some big news on you and then died. Without giving you the chance to ask questions or process what she said. And that hurts."

Tears ran down Helene's face, but she didn't bother wiping them. Guilt washed over her about Grammy and her death. What if she hadn't left the house that day? Maybe she and Grammy could have talked through things. Or, at the very least, she could have been there to call the ambulance and to stay with Pappy while he waited. If she hadn't been so hurt and selfish, Pappy might have lived. There was a chance he could have met his great-granddaughter.

Maybe she couldn't have saved either one of them, but at least she would have tried. That was the real reason she'd changed. Dr. Austen was right. Holding onto the pain from a decision made decades ago still impacted her today.

Not only her life, but everyone around her. How unfair was it that Max had spent their entire marriage accommodating her when all she had to do was take a step back and acknowledge her mistake? It might even be natural to react the way she did. The problem was she was still reacting.

Shaking her head, Helene calculated how much time she'd wasted. It was a wonder Max hadn't exploded years ago from dealing with her issues.

As if Dr. Austen could read her mind, the therapist said, "Max initiated changes on his part to take more control of his life, but he didn't complete the process before he collapsed." Dr. Austen paused while Helene blew her nose. "You're guilty of a lot of things. But not for causing Max's incident or killing your grandmother. It's clear, though, why you've never wanted to talk about your family."

"So . . . Max doesn't hate me?" Helene hated the immature feeling she had, but she couldn't help herself. She needed to know if her past was going to alter how her husband saw her. "I feel ridiculous asking you when I should know the answer."

"Do you think someone who hated you would go to the lengths Max has to improve himself? You know he's been seeing me since Sara moved to Chicago. He didn't know how to comfort either of you, so he sought out help, which is something you should do when you don't know how to deal with a situation." The therapist gave Helene a half grin. "I trust you understand that now."

Helene grinned back. "Yes. Thank you." The smile faded as Helene considered the actions she needed to reveal to her family and therapist. Hesitantly, she asked, "What's the best way to come clean about all the really demanding things I've done?"

"I advise my clients to rip off the bandage. It hurts, but it's quick."

"But that's just for my feelings, right? Being honest with Max and the girls doesn't ensure they'll forgive me for the things I did. Even though I did them with their interest in mind."

"Are you sure?" Dr. Austen asked as she rolled her pen between her fingers. "Is that really how you see things?"

Letting out a shaky breath, Helene remembered what Max had said to her before he collapsed. *It took thirty-seven years for this situation to evolve. Why can't you take this seriously? It's not a joke.*

Helene nodded. "A few weeks ago, yes. I would have. But you're right. All of it was for me. I spent most of our marriage focused on what *I* wanted, not what Max desired."

Dr. Austen gave her a smile. "So, with that in mind, remember: confessing your shortcomings is for you and you alone. There's no way of knowing whether you will be forgiven."

Helene closed her eyes and took in a deep breath. She couldn't go on with this much guilt on her conscience. Grammy may be dead, but Max, Sara, and Tasha were alive and would be for years to come. She'd made a mess of her friends and acquaintances, but she had a chance to fix it if she acted now.

A cloud of doubt washed over her. What if her family wouldn't accept her change? What if it was too late? Then she really would be all alone—the abandoned girl no one wanted.

"Stop the stinkin' thinkin' right now, Helene," she muttered to herself. "It's not getting you anywhere. It's almost as bad as wanting to be in control all the time."

Helene opened her eyes to Dr. Austen staring at her.

"I don't know where that came from," said Dr. Austen, "but it's not bad advice."

Unable to sit still, Helene leaned down to pull out her compact from her purse. She opened it and flinched at the sight of her red, puffy eyes. Helene powdered the damage to her face.

"Grammy used to say that," Helene said as she dabbed at her face. "I think that might be my best memory of her. The times when she was positive and helpful. Maybe she wanted to be that way all the time, but it's harder than it looks. I know from firsthand experience."

"Do you have anything else you need to get off your chest, Helene? Something tells me Max isn't the only person you've attempted to control."

Helene clicked her compact shut and dropped it into her purse. "We may need an entire day for my confession," she said, and laughed. When Dr. Austen didn't join in, Helene cleared her throat. "Okay. Fine. Yes, Sara and Tasha have been the focus of some of my more strenuous control-seeking endeavors. In fact, I've been planning Tasha's wedding for her. She found a gorgeous dress, and the venue will be magnificent—"

"Did she ask for your help?" Dr. Austen interrupted.

Helene twisted her wedding ring so that the solitaire was centered in the middle of her finger. "Not at first. But then the wedding dress she wanted was discontinued, and she couldn't find it anywhere . . ." Helene trailed off. If she wasn't honest with Dr. Austen, how was she going to be honest with her daughter? "Well, that's not quite true. I might have had something do to with that too."

She explained about the dozen wedding dresses hidden in the closet of the guest room as well as her calls to *The Gazette* to secure the "Wedding of the Year" feature. While she was at it, she confessed to making sure her granddaughter's dress was the color she wanted, the cake samples from the bakery she preferred, and the photographer the one Eveline Gerome had wanted for her anniversary party but couldn't get.

The words flowed out of her mouth, and, with them, the knot in her stomach loosened. The relief didn't last long, though. When Dr. Austen didn't immediately speak, Helene glanced over. The therapist sat there, staring straight ahead.

While Helene preferred silence to probing questions, the look on the therapist's face made her nervous.

"Are you okay?" asked Helene.

"Do you have any idea what you've done?"

The knot in Helene's stomach tightened, sending a spasm through her body. "I confessed all the things I've done in hopes of controlling my family."

"That too. But you went way past control, Helene. This is manipulation on a major scale. What do you suppose is going to happen if Tasha finds out what you've done?"

Helene hesitated. She'd never once considered how her daughter would feel. She'd done what she thought was the right thing in order to have the best wedding dress possible. It never occurred to her that the ends didn't justify the means. Bile worked its way up her throat. "Oh my God. I am a horrible person, aren't I?"

"Horrible might be a bit much, but you have some work to do." Dr. Austen leaned forward. "Today, you've admitted your mistakes to yourself. You've also acknowledged that no one else has to forgive you for what you did. There isn't a magic wand or incantation to make this go away. You're going to have to work for it. Are you ready to do that?"

Helene straightened her back and nodded. "Absolutely. What should I do?"

25

"Gin! I told you being bedridden wasn't going to impact my ability to beat you!" Max smiled at his eldest daughter. He knew how much she hated to lose, but he couldn't help it. "We could play again if you want a rematch."

Sara gathered up the cards and slid them back into their box. "No, thank you. That was the third and final time I'm going to let you humiliate me today. Maybe tomorrow. After I've had time to lick my wounds." She checked her watch. "Mom should be back anytime. I'll head out now."

Max had hoped he could keep Sara around long enough for her to run into Helene. He'd learned a few tricks from his wife over the years that would help him convince Sara to stay. He preferred to use them only when it was absolutely necessary, but desperate times called for desperate measures. Sara had been in town for six days and planned to return to Chicago on Saturday. Time was running out for a reconciliation between mother and daughter on this trip. He decided to take the bull by the horns.

"You're going to have to talk to her at some point, you know."

His daughter flashed a grim smile. "I wondered how long it would take for you to start in on that. Tasha and I made a bet, actually."

Pushing himself up against the pillows, Max kept his face neutral. His younger daughter had confessed to the bet earlier in the week but hadn't told him the outcome.

"Who won?" asked Max. Based on what he knew about the girls, he suspected Tasha would be the winner, but he wanted to hear it from Sara.

"She did. But you already knew that, didn't you?" Sara asked as she leaned against the doorframe.

"I had my suspicions, but it never hurts to get the facts. As an attorney, you know that."

Crossing her arms over her chest, Sara pursed her lips before she spoke. "Is that supposed to be a hint that it's my turn to get the facts from Mom about why she's been such a pain in the ass?"

Max nodded. "Yeah. Though you and I both know she wouldn't appreciate—"

"My language," Sara interrupted. "Yes, I'm well aware." She rolled her eyes as she walked back to the bed and sat down next to her father. "The adult part of me knows I need to be mature about this and give her another chance. But the daughter version of me is still pissed. She really was manipulative and rude. How many people do you know who force a relationship coordinator on their children?"

"Wasn't there a movie about that a few years back? The actor who played the bongos wouldn't move out of his parents' house, and they hired someone to figure out how to get him to leave."

She laughed, and Max knew they were making progress.

"Dad, that movie's fifteen years old by now. And it's fiction.

It isn't supposed to happen in real life." She leaned in and kissed him. "I've really got to go. Jared needs me to do some work on a project, and I've still got a few hours of research to do before our conference call later." She stood up. "Do you need anything else before I go?"

Using the last stall tactic he had saved up, Max nodded. "Yes. Could you go into the guest room and look in the closet? I've got a box of old Louis L'Amour books stashed in there. Your mother keeps forgetting to bring them to me." He picked up a book on the nightstand. "She thinks these how-to manuals about reducing stress and eating healthy are better for me than a good ol' Western."

"Fine. I'll do that, then I'm out of here."

He watched as his daughter left the room, then he noticed his cell phone was blinking. A missed call and a voicemail. In all the excitement of the card game, he hadn't noticed Helene had called.

Max listened to the message and learned Helene had decided to stop for coffee before she came home and wouldn't be back for another hour.

"Well, that's convenient, isn't it?" Max muttered to himself. It looked like neither his wife nor daughter wanted to run into each other. He looked up in time to see Sara hefting a box through the doorway. He wasn't sure if it was the box or something else that had her frowning.

"Why didn't you tell me this thing was so heavy?" Max felt the mattress lurch when Sara dropped the box on the foot of the bed. "I don't think Mom forgot about the books. She just didn't want to lug them in here."

"I guess that makes sense too." He held up his phone. "Your mother's going to be late. Apparently, she detoured for coffee on her way home. We've got time for another round of rummy."

"Sorry, I've got to go." She opened the box, and a poof of dust blew up. Waving her arms to clear the air, she added, "I'll call tomorrow, and you can tell me about your adventures in the Wild West."

She gave him a kiss, then walked out of the room. He reached down to pull the box closer to him and rummaged through it. It wasn't until the front door closed that he remembered what else was in the closet with the box of books: the discontinued wedding dresses Helene had purchased to keep Tasha from finding them.

"Damn it, Max," he said as he scurried out of bed and shuffled as fast as he could to the front door. "What were you thinking?"

He needed to catch Sara before she left. If Sara told her sister what she'd found, Helene's problems would multiply. But by the time he got to the front door, Sara's car was already down the street. Max checked the pockets of his pajamas but remembered his phone was still in the bedroom.

Feeling out of breath from all the rushing around, he plopped down in a living room chair and rested his head in his hands. As much as he wanted Helene to come clean about the dresses, the last thing he meant to do was out her accidentally. He tried to push himself out of the chair to return to the bedroom, but a sense of panic and exhaustion came over him.

"Come on, Maxwell. You can do this. You're not an old man, and the doctor said you're fine. Relax."

The pep talk didn't seem to work, as he had a hard time catching his breath. He forced himself to inhale deeply through his nose and exhale slowly out his mouth. He might be aging and infirm, but he still had a job to do.

"I can do this," Max muttered as he forced himself out of the chair and limped back to the bedroom. He needed to get that box of books back to the closet before Helene got home. He also needed to figure out how to let his wife know her secret was out.

26

"That will be $5.23, please."

Helene's hand shook slightly as she dug into her purse for her wallet. She hated spending this much money on a cup of coffee, but after her session with Dr. Austen, she needed some time to calm down.

Handing the barista some cash, Helene moved to the pickup station to wait for her order. This was something else she didn't understand. Coffee wasn't that difficult to make. Even with the hundreds of varieties of drinks, it shouldn't take more than a few minutes to serve.

She counted each minute as she waited for her caffeine. At least it was a distraction from the huge confessions she would have to make when she went home to see Max.

"Pumpkin spice latte for Helen," called out another barista.

"It's Helene," she corrected the young woman, who pushed her overgrown bangs with a hot-pink streak out of her face. "My name is Helene."

The girl nodded. "Did you have a pumpkin spice latte?"

Helene nodded back.

"Okay, then. That's your drink."

Before she had a chance to explain the importance of good customer service, Helene heard someone call her name, pronounced properly. The familiar voice might have gotten her name right, but all she wanted to do was hightail it out of the store.

"I know you can hear me," said Eveline Gerome. "I'm standing right behind you."

Helene picked up her latte, plastered a smile on her face, and turned toward Tasha's ex-mother-in-law. "Eveline. What a surprise to see you here."

"Not really. This is the closest coffee shop to that dreadful therapist's office. I figured you'd show up sooner or later."

Eveline turned, and Helene watched her walk toward a table in the corner of the shop. As she settled into one of the chairs, Eveline looked up and frowned. "Well, hurry up. I don't have all day."

Standing tall in preparation for whatever happened next, Helene marched to the corner and sat opposite Eveline. She put her purse next to her on a chair and placed the hot coffee down with only a slight tremble. Unsure what Eveline wanted, Helene twisted her wedding band and waited.

"How is Max?"

Small talk. Great. Funny how the one person I don't want to spend time around wants to chat.

"He's fine. Thank you for asking." She reached for her coffee and took a sip. The liquid burned her throat, making her wince. She'd forgotten how hot the coffee was here. Glancing up, she caught Eveline observing her. Like how Blake watched an ant under a magnifying glass. Between the coffee and the hot flash she felt coming on, Helene didn't need any more heat. "Is there something I can do for you?"

"Direct. At least you have that going for you." Eveline crossed her arms over her chest. "Why are you following me to Dr. Austen's?"

Helene's eyebrows shot up. "I'm not."

"Really? You just happen to show up every week at the same time I'm there?"

This explains where Doug got his intelligence. His mother doesn't understand the concept of appointments.

"My appointment is at eleven on Wednesdays. I see Dr. Austen every week." She cleared her throat. "Except for last week."

"Because of Max's thing. Roger told me about that. I always knew Max wouldn't last long. He doesn't have the strong genes my Roger has," she said, a smile appearing on her face. "Hopefully that will balance out Blake's bad genetics."

Not interested in getting into an argument about whose husband was better, Helene looked at her watch. "I have fifteen minutes before I need to leave. My preference is to spend it alone in peace and quiet. Do you need something or are you just being obtuse? I think that runs in your family, too, if memory serves. Doug wasn't the brightest bulb on the string."

Helene gave herself a mental fist bump when she saw her approach startled Eveline. She still didn't know what was going on, but she refused to let the other woman get the best of her.

Eveline leaned forward and wiggled her index finger at Helene, indicating that she come closer.

Helene sat forward and waited.

"Whatever you're up to, it won't work. I'm not letting you take Roger away from me."

Eveline's comment took Helene by surprise. Here she was, struggling to hang onto her own marriage and needing to do some major repair work on her relationship with her daughters. She didn't have the time or energy to mess with anyone else, not that Eveline needed to know that.

When she had her emotions under control, Helene said, "I don't know what you're talking about. Max and I are happy, and even if we weren't, Roger is the last person I would turn to." She couldn't help but add, "But I can't speak for Roger. Maybe he's tired of putting up with you."

Fear crept into Eveline's eyes for a second before the woman pushed back her chair. She moved so fast the chair rammed into the barista who was delivering drinks at the table behind them. The cups on the tray fell to the floor, and coffee splattered everywhere. Lucky to be out of the splatter radius, Helene watched as Eveline frantically wiped the liquid off her fake Birkin bag.

"How clumsy can you get?" shrieked Eveline. "It's your job to carry coffee, not drop it all over people!"

The girl with the pink hair looked up from the ground where she was picking up the empty cups and tray. "It's not my job to dodge chairs that people push into me. You caused the accident. Don't scream at *me*."

"You've ruined my bag," Eveline whined. "Look at it. Coffee stains leather. Do you know how much this bag cost?"

Blowing her bangs out of her face, the girl said, "One, I didn't ruin it. Two, the bag's not real leather. And three, too much." The girl loaded up the trash and looked at the couple whose drinks were ruined. "Sorry about that. I'll go remake your order. Just give me a minute."

Helene sat back and listened while Eveline ranted about the incompetencies of the customer service industry while she scrubbed at the spots on her bag with a napkin. It occurred to Helene that Eveline had forgotten she was even sitting there. Imagine that. The woman accused her of trying to steal her husband, then forgot all about it because of a coffee spill. Eveline was more self-centered than she was.

She took a sip of her own coffee, now a little cooler than before, and wondered if this was how her daughters saw her. An involuntary shudder ran down her back. Her behavior in the past with Sara was just as ridiculous as Eveline's was today.

Memories of the times she thought she was "helping" flooded back to her.

"Ask your sister to pay off your law school loans. She won the lottery."

"How on God's green earth did you put on shoes that don't match?"

"Every woman needs a husband, so I signed you up with a relationship coordinator."

As if those weren't bad enough, she finally understood why Sara had had to leave town. Helene was jealous of the fact that Sara felt more comfortable asking Betty for help than she did her own mother. If there was one thing in the world she could take back, it was the words she had spoken to Sara that day at Betty's Coffee Bar: *"Anyone as hard-hearted as you is not easy to love."*

Eveline's voice broke through Helene's revelation as she yelled at the barista who was back with the refills.

"I should get free coffee here for the rest of my life after what you've done to my purse!"

The girl ignored Eveline while she apologized to the couple again for the delay. At first, Helene thought the girl was going to go back to the counter, but she stopped at their table and addressed Helene.

"I don't know you, but I do have some advice." She pointed at Eveline. "You don't want to be anything like this woman. It's my experience that people who are mean to people they don't know are even meaner to the people they *do* know. Get out while you can."

With that, the barista stomped off, leaving Eveline with her mouth hanging open and Helene in awe that someone so young could understand a truth she was only beginning to comprehend.

The girl was right. Helene had learned her behavior from Grammy, who had picked it up as a defense mechanism when

Doris died. Helene had been so concerned with following Grammy's example that she had failed to notice she was pushing everyone away. Just like Grammy had done to her.

Before she could change her mind, Helene grabbed her bag and her coffee. "I'm going home. Max is waiting for me, and I have no interest in hearing any more of the garbage you're spewing."

Helene took off for the door. As it closed behind her, she heard Eveline call out, "You can't talk to me like that! I will make your life a living hell!"

Gritting her teeth, Helene shook her head. "It can't be any worse than what I did to myself."

27

Sitting at the kitchen table, Helene reviewed the list she and Dr. Austen had made the day before. Helene glanced at the first few items on it. They were simple and shouldn't take long. Dr. Austen conceded she could use the first few apologies as a warm-up.

"I'd prefer you dive right in, but if it makes you more comfortable to practice before you talk to your daughters, then go ahead. At least you can use those interactions to show your daughters you're serious about changing."

Helene scrunched up her nose as she sipped her coffee. The pumpkin pie latte from yesterday made her home-brewed cup less appealing, but she wanted to keep her eye on Max. He had been out of bed when she got home after her coffee run-in with Eveline.

She'd texted Sara as soon as she'd returned him to bed.

When you left Dad, where was he?

She didn't want to accuse her daughter of not taking care of Max, but Helene needed to know. There wasn't any reason for him to get out of bed, but when she'd asked him about it, Max was tight-lipped.

"I took a walk around the house," he'd said. "I got tired of the bedroom and wanted to see something else. The doctor said I should get some exercise."

Sara's response was what she expected.

In bed. Why?

Not wanting to worry or set off Sara, Helene chewed on her lip to come up with an acceptable answer. If Sara thought she was accusing her of something, that would not help their relationship. She focused on giving resolution in her text.

No reason. Just curious.

Her response must have satisfied her daughter, because the next text Sara sent was on a different topic.

Heading back to Chicago Saturday. I'll say goodbye to Dad before I leave.

It irritated Helene that Sara didn't want to say goodbye to her, but as hard as it was to bite her tongue, chastising her daughter would be a mistake Helene didn't want to repeat. She needed to focus on her list.

Shaking off her nerves, Helene called Cynthia at *The Gazette* and explained she wanted to remove the request for the "Wedding of the Year" nomination.

"No one in the history of Glen Valley has done that, Mrs. Shaw. Are you feeling okay? I heard your husband just had a stroke. Is the stress of taking care of him getting to you?" the young reporter asked.

"It wasn't a stroke, dear. Just a medical event. He's fine now. But I'm serious about the contest. Tasha isn't interested, and I've no right to interfere in her wedding."

"Now I've heard it all," Cynthia mumbled before she added, "I'll take you off the list, then. For the life of me, I don't know why Tasha wouldn't be thrilled to be in the running. But it's your call."

Ignoring Cynthia's dig at her requested change, Helene thanked the woman, hung up the phone, and continued down her list of to-dos. She giggled when she recognized the list was actually "un-dos."

"I haven't heard you giggle like that since we were in high school," Max said as he wandered into the kitchen.

She glanced at him and forced herself not to walk over and help him to the table. He looked frail, and it frightened her. Now that she'd figured out what had gotten her to this point in her life and was ready to address it, the things outside of her control made her feel even more helpless.

"Why don't you giggle like that more?" Max asked when he finally sat down on the kitchen stool next to hers. She let him catch his breath before she answered.

"Giggling isn't very adult, now, is it?" she said. She held up her hand when he started to speak. "I know, I know. I will relax a bit, but that doesn't mean I have to revert to childishness."

Max wrapped his arm around her shoulders. Her arm tingled when his fingers touched her bare skin.

"I don't recall being a child in high school. The stuff we did was a little more TV-MA."

She blushed as she thought about some of the times they'd stolen away together under the pretext of studying. Several times they'd almost been caught, but somehow, they'd always escaped the notice of Max's parents.

"You know," Max said as he nodded to the kitchen door, "we could always go to the bedroom for a refresher."

"Maxwell Howard Shaw! What has gotten into you lately?"

"All those fresh fruits and vegetables you've been feeding me." He kissed her neck. "We have all day."

Helene wondered if her cheeks could get any hotter. Thankful that her husband found her attractive after all these years, and after all the mistakes she'd made, she gave him a peck on the cheek and stood up. The look on his face reminded her of the look he gave her in high school when she put a stop to things.

"Remember when you told me you wanted to spend the rest of your life with me?"

Max grinned. "Like it was yesterday. We were studying for a World History test. You moved away from me then, too, remember?"

The image of Max's childhood bedroom filled her head.

Farrah Fawcett smiled down from her poster above Max's bed while *The Godfather* movie poster glared at them from his closet door.

"Max, we have to study."

Rolling his eyes, Max took her hand and kissed it. "I know, but you are so beautiful, I can't keep my hands off you." He continued kissing her arm, moving up until he got to her neck. His warm breath tickled, and she giggled. "And clearly, you're enjoying it too."

Lowering her head to hide her neck, she leaned away from Max. If he kept kissing her like that, the history test they were studying for would be forgotten. And if she wanted Grammy to agree to let her go to prom, she needed an A on this test.

Helene grabbed her textbook and stood up.

"Hey, where're you going? You don't have to be home for another hour."

"To the other side of the room," she said as she sat down on the beanbag chair below his dart board. It was her second favorite place to sit when she was at Max's house. Her first favorite place wasn't helping her get any studying done. "You'll be fine if you don't study, but I'm not as smart as you. I have to spend more time learning this."

Max frowned from the couch. "Why do you talk yourself down so much? You're just as smart as I am. The only reason you're having problems is because you moved around so much.

It isn't your fault that your last school didn't teach World History and now you have to catch up."

Opening her book again, Helene said, "It may not be my fault, but if I don't figure this out by tomorrow, I'll never hear the end of it."

The room was silent for a moment, and Helene looked over at Max. She watched his eyebrows raise, which told her he was contemplating something. She didn't have to wait long to find out what it was.

"Why do you let her bother you like that?"

Helene didn't have to ask whom he was talking about. The last thing she wanted to discuss was her grandmother. They'd spent too much time talking about the woman who made her life miserable. She loved spending time with Max, and her future was with him, but his need to have her get along with her grandmother was frustrating.

"Not everyone gets along with their parents."

"They aren't your parents."

Another subject they avoided.

Max didn't wait for her response. "The only person hurting you is her. I don't know why you can't see that."

"Don't start in on Grammy. She gave up a lot when she and Pappy took me in. You can't blame her for trying to protect me."

"Protect you? I wouldn't call it that. Tearing you down, maybe. Bullying, yes. Protecting? Not so much."

Struggling to hold back tears, Helene stared down at the page. A pencil sketch of a victim of the bubonic plague looked back at her. As if her own life weren't depressing enough, this week's lesson highlighted the millions of Europeans who had died in the 1300s from something invisible carried by a flea.

Max pulled the textbook out of her hands and drew her to her feet. "I'm sorry." He wrapped his arms around her and pulled her close. Despite her frustration, she relaxed into him, letting his warmth absorb the cold sadness she always felt about her grandmother. "I don't like it when we fight."

"I don't either," she said. "But there are certain things I can't change. Like who I live with."

"Someday you'll be able to make that decision. Maybe you'll even agree to marry me, and we can live happily ever after."

Helene's eyes widened. She'd always wished for a fairy tale, but she didn't dream about it. At least not while she was still in high school.

Stepping back, Helene stared up at Max. He looked serious, but did he really know what he was offering her?

"You want to spend your life with me?"

Leaning in, Max kissed her gently on the lips before he said, "Of course I do. I love you. And I want you to be happy."

Helene kept staring. She'd known in her heart that Max was the one, but they'd never talked about it. Now she knew Max loved her and wanted her as his wife. What would Grammy think of that?

The familiar dread spread through her as she imagined her grandmother's reaction. For so long, Grammy had told her not to expect much. She wasn't the smartest or prettiest, and her past would drive away even the strongest men. Helene wondered why Grammy always seemed embarrassed about raising her granddaughter, but right now, it didn't matter. Someone else loved her for her.

Taking a deep breath, Helene brushed her lips on Max's cheek, then stepped back. "Thank you. I love you too, and I want to talk about our future. But before we can do that, I really need to pass World History. Can we keep studying?" She held her breath, hoping Max would understand her need to focus on the present before they dealt with the future.

Much to her relief, Max tugged her toward the beanbag. "Sit down and we'll go through the chapter again."

28

"What grade did you get in World History?"

Max's question startled her back to reality.

"An A. Thanks to you!" Helene glanced at the clock on the kitchen wall. "Right now, I have enough time to make a few more phone calls." She pointed at the list in front of Max. "That's my *un-do* list. I told Dr. Austen I'd fix as much as I could before this week's session. The baker needs to be set straight, and I need to talk to the florist. I might have gone overboard with my last order."

Max nodded. "That's an interesting name for a list." He looked down at the page and frowned. "The dresses aren't on here."

Immediately on alert, she asked, "How do you know about the dresses?"

Max's face pinked. "You never brought me the Louis L'Amour books like I asked. The box was stuffed behind the dresses."

"Oh. Well, if you'll notice, it is on the list of things *to* do." She pointed to the page before she continued. "But I've decided to take that secret to the grave. Tasha is so happy with her wedding dress. So is Libby with the junior bridesmaid's dress. Or maid of honor gown, if Sara doesn't come to her senses." Max frowned, and Helene corrected herself. "I mean if I don't apologize and ask her to come to the wedding. But if I tell Tasha what I did, it would spoil everything."

"She already knows."

Max spoke the words so softly that Helene thought she misheard. She looked at him and was reminded again of how much he'd aged in the last week. A deep furrow settled into his forehead, and his jowls sagged almost below his jawline. It reminded her of the movie she'd watched with Libby and Blake, where the beautiful mother of the heroine was unveiled to be a wicked witch and aged a thousand years in just a few seconds.

"What do you mean?"

Standing up from the stool, Max stumbled in his haste. "Sara saw all the dresses in the closet yesterday." For a second, he looked like Blake did when he took another chocolate chip cookie after being told no. "She brought me the box of L'Amour books from the guest closet. I forgot the dresses were in there when I asked her."

"How did the books get back to the closet?" Helene suspected his answer had something to do with why she had found him on the floor.

Max shuffled to the cabinet and pulled out a glass. He poured himself some water from the faucet and drank it before he answered. Helene noticed his hand shook a little when he set the glass on the counter.

"I put the books back."

Helene leaned forward and opened her mouth to speak, but Max raised his hand.

"Let me explain. I knew you'd be upset, and I wanted to figure out a way to defuse the situation without causing more problems."

She sat back and nodded. Her husband was right. She would have been furious if she'd known Sara, and probably Tasha, knew what she'd done, but her first reaction would have been to deny she'd done anything wrong. Helene sighed. She was so predictable.

"When you got home and told me about your run-in with Eveline, you were so calm. It surprised me. That woman knows how to push people's buttons, especially yours. And for her to accuse you of wanting Roger? I'm shocked you didn't deck her." Max walked back to her and put his hand on her shoulder. "But you handled it. Better than usual. And maybe that's why I didn't tell you then about the books. You'd already dealt with Eveline's crap, and I was passed out on the floor. By the way, you blamed Sara for that, didn't you?"

She blushed and looked down at the floor when she understood how well her husband knew her. Max's finger tipped up her chin. Her heart sped up when she saw the love in his eyes.

"I'm sorry I didn't tell you yesterday. I know you and Dr. Austen are working through things, but can you have patience with me? I'm going to have to get used to the improved Helene Shaw."

Her throat swelled, and tears threatened to spill from her eyes. She stared back at her husband while she collected herself.

Once she was calm, she said, "Of course I'll be patient, but I'm not perfect. Remember what I said to Eveline yesterday?"

Max leaned in and pressed his lips to hers. She wanted to fall into the kiss, but she needed to tell Max what she'd learned the day before. Pushing back on his shoulders, Helene pulled away, and he smiled.

"I'd rather kiss you than hear what you said, but I'm guessing this is something I need to hear."

"Eveline didn't like that I stood up to her, and she's going to be difficult. I can't prevent that. But there is nothing she or anyone else can do to me that's worse than what I've already done to myself. I've got a long way to go." Helene took a deep breath before she continued. "You have to tell me when my selfishness affects you. I couldn't bear if I killed someone else because of my actions."

Relief coursed through her veins as the words left her mouth. But it was short-lived when she saw the look on Max's face.

"What is that supposed to mean? You haven't killed anyone. Irritated the living daylights out of me, but I'm still kicking."

Helene realized she'd never told Max about her conversation with Dr. Austen. She'd planned to, but when she found him on the floor of the hallway, other things took precedence. He needed to know the truth about her parents and Grammy, but she hesitated. Getting back to full strength should be Max's focus, not the fact that she'd warped her childhood memories and made them into adult-sized dysfunctional nightmares.

"Out with it, Helene. No more secrets."

The gruff sound of Max's voice jolted her back to the present.

"Yes, I'm scared you're going to die. And you would be too if the situation were reversed." She held up her hand when Max started to speak. "You need to hear everything Dr. Austen and I discussed yesterday. Then I'll call Tasha and Sara and fix this." Looking Max in the eyes, Helene said, "I killed Grammy."

Max shook his head. "Your grandmother had a stroke, Helene. You didn't cause that."

She gently covered his mouth with her hand. "Please. Can I just explain this?"

She felt Max's cool lips pucker and kiss her palm. Then he took her hand in his and pulled her gently to the living room where he sat down on the couch. He tugged her to follow him, but she shook her head and pulled her hand from his.

"I need to stand up to say this. I'm too nervous to sit down."

Helene waited until Max settled into the pillows before she started her story.

"Grammy and I argued before she died. We'd been talking about naming Sara after my parents, and she opposed the idea. Her head hurt, and I followed her into the bathroom, badgering her about it, and she finally lost her temper and told me the truth about my parents."

Max sighed when he said, "That your dad was drunk the night your parents died in the car accident?"

The room tilted, and Helene's vision blacked out for a second. She heard Max's voice in the distance as he called out, but all she could do was let her body catch up from the shock that Max knew about her parents.

Pressure on her upper arms led her someplace, and she felt herself being pushed down. The couch cushions nestled under her back, and Max tucked a throw pillow under her knees. She heard Max leave the room, only to return a minute later.

"Sit up and drink some water."

She did as she was told, the cool water wetting her parched throat as she swallowed. Relieved that the room didn't spin, and her vision and hearing seemed back to normal, she turned and sat up against the back of the couch.

"So, I can still shock you, can I?" Max asked with a grin.

"Apparently so." She took another sip of water before she asked, "How did you know?"

"Pappy told me."

The room spun again, and Helene closed her eyes. She took another sip of water before peeking at Max through squinting eyes. "When?"

"Prom night. Our senior year."

"You've known for thirty-nine years and never thought about telling me?" She wanted to storm out of the room, but she didn't have the energy. The remaining water in the glass shook as she put it on the table, not even bothering to put it on a coaster. "How could you stand to be around me, knowing this? I'm a terrible person. We never should have had a family. What if Sara or Tasha had turned out like my father?"

"Helene, this isn't about you. Your father had an illness he couldn't control. Your mom was in the wrong place at the wrong time," said Max as he sat down next to her. "Our family turned out fine. It may not have been exactly what you wanted, but by most standards, we did okay."

She didn't have the energy to argue, but she needed to know. "Tell me."

"Tell you what?" Max asked.

Lying her head on Max's shoulder, Helene closed her eyes. "What did Pappy tell you?"

29

"Do you remember your prom dress?" Max asked Helene. The conversation about Pappy would be difficult, so he wanted to make sure Helene knew how much he loved her. "I couldn't keep my eyes off you."

"You were a hormonal eighteen-year-old boy. I was wearing a polka-dot dress that got remade into curtains for our first apartment. Sounds a little pathetic to me."

"Stop!" Max shouted, then regretted his tone when he saw Helene flinch. He said in a softer tone, "Don't do that to yourself. Or to me. Stop being negative. You are better than that. Let me show you."

Taking her hand, he recalled prom night.

MAX LOOKED AT HELENE, her head resting against the passenger side headrest of the Camaro Z28, bobbing along to the Bee Gees' "How Deep is Your Love" on the radio. It had been a great night, even if he had to wear a tuxedo. The light-blue jacket lay in the back seat, and he tugged at the collar of the starched blue dress shirt.

He would do it again, monkey suit and all, to see Helene this happy. He glanced over again, and she smiled back.

Tonight, Helene had clicked with everyone. The evening went off without a hitch, and everyone got to see Helene at the top of her game. They'd shared dinner with twelve other couples at the only Italian restaurant in the county, danced to some disco tunes in the tissue-paper-camouflaged high school gymnasium, and cheered Eveline Hardy and Roger Gerome when they won prom queen and king.

Max couldn't have asked for a better end to the evening. Now he just needed to get her home and talk to Pappy about his marriage proposal before he left. The perfect end to the perfect prom.

"What are you thinking about over there? You seem pretty proud of yourself. Is it because you didn't get any marinara sauce on your shirt, so you get your deposit back?"

Leave it to Helene to think about money at a time like this.

Shaking his head, he said, "I'm happy, that's all."

They continued the rest of the drive in a pleasant silence. Max hoped Helene didn't get suspicious that he wasn't talking. He normally carried their conversations, but he was nervous about the proposal. What if Pappy said no?

Max turned the car into the driveway of Helene's grandparents' house and slowly inched the Z28 up the drive.

"Scared of the potholes?" Helene asked.

Scared of Pappy's response, thought Max, but he said instead, "Yeah. I don't want to cause any damage. Frank and I just fixed the scrapes from when I drove it to check out colleges."

As soon as the words left his mouth, Max knew he'd said the wrong thing. Helene couldn't afford college and was still upset he planned to go. He wanted to explain that getting a college education was vital in his plan to marry and support her and their family, but he didn't want to get into that discussion tonight.

Apparently neither did she because, instead of speaking, she laid her head on the headrest and waited quietly until he parked. Before he turned off the headlights, he noticed something moving on the porch of the old house.

"Pappy waited up," Helene murmured.

Max nodded but kept silent. He knew her grandfather had made tonight happen. Her grandmother thought prom was a waste of time and money, but Pappy had stood his ground.

"I'll walk you up," said Max. Helene reached for the door handle, but Max put out his hand. "No, I'll get it. Wait a second."

He reached into the back seat and grabbed his coat. Shrugging into it after he crawled out of the Z28, he walked to the passenger side of the car and opened the door for Helene. He bowed with a flourish and held out his hand. "My lady. Home before curfew."

As he escorted her to the porch, Max heard the unmistakable sound of Pappy's side-by-side snapping closed.

"Damn good thing too," Pappy called from the porch. The shotgun's silhouette stood out against the house. "I was ready for ya if you were late with my granddaughter."

The porch light caught the twinkle in Helene's eye.

"He sounds drunk. Sorry about that. This whole prom thing got to him. Grammy ignored him for the last two weeks. He's had to make his own supper."

"I'm not drunk, just a little loose. 'Sides, canned anchovies get old after a while," Pappy said. "Come on up here, you two. I wanna take 'nother look at ya."

Helene hesitated. Max knew she was self-conscious of her grandparents, but he didn't want her to worry. He loved her regardless of her family. Max tugged gently on her hand tucked under his elbow.

"Let's go talk to Pappy."

"Damn straight you're gonna talk to Pappy!" Pappy hiccupped before he asked, "How was it?"

Helene floated up the stairs next to Max, then broke away and twirled her way to where Pappy sat. "It was a dream come true! Thank you, Pappy, for everything you did. You are my fairy grandfather!" She kissed his weathered and wrinkled cheek. "I couldn't ask for anything else."

Taking a sip from his drink, Pappy said, "You should, but I'm happy you're happy." His eyes narrowed as he looked between the two of them. "It's time to say good night. I ain't havin' a perfect evening spoiled with some teenage shenanigans."

Max felt his face heat up at the same time he saw Helene's cheeks flush. Pappy's routine insinuations always embarrassed them. It didn't make sense why he was so vocal about stuff like that, but considering what Max planned to ask Pappy before he left, he knew he should get used to it.

Knowing the routine, Max took Helene's hand and kissed it before she kissed his cheek and danced into the house. He watched her blue dress twirl around her as she spun into the house and closed the door softly behind her. Max felt Pappy's eyes bore into him like they did every time he brought Helene home.

The difference tonight was that he was about to do something that would deserve Pappy's ire.

Max turned toward the old man and nodded at the double barrel. "You know, you can stop sitting out here with that thing every time I come by. I'd never do anything to hurt her."

Pappy flicked a switch on the side of the gun with his thumb, and the barrel dropped open.

"It's empty. It's always empty," said Pappy as he snapped up the gun and set it to the side. He grabbed his glass again and took another sip. "Mostly show. I thought you'd have figured it out by now."

Pointing to the chair next to Pappy, Max asked, "May I sit down?"

"Course." The old man pointed at his glass. "You want some hooch? Been saving this bottle for a while. Only break it out on special occasions."

Max shook his head. "No, thanks, Mr. Parker, I'm—"

"It's Pappy, son. We've talked about that before. You're a smart man, so I know you heard me." He took another sip. "Do you want to know what the occasion is tonight?"

He was too nervous to really care what Pappy was reminiscing about. Asking his permission to marry Helene was the priority at the moment, but Max understood that when an adult asked him a question, he answered.

"Is it prom, sir? Helene looked beautiful tonight. And I should thank you again for helping her with the dress. She told me you paid for the material."

Pappy harrumphed. "Least I could do. She and her grammy get along like fire and water. Just like her momma and grammy did."

Not sure what to say to that, Max remained silent. He knew Helene's parents had died young, but she never talked about them. As far as he knew, no one talked about them.

"Doris." Pappy paused. "That was Helene's momma. Her name was Doris."

Max nodded. "Nice name."

"Yeah, it was, wasn't it?" Pappy gazed out into the yard, although Max was sure he couldn't see anything. It reminded him of the way his own mother acted when she thought about something sad. "Anyway, Doris didn't go to the prom. Did ya know that? She was too busy with her baby. Helene was—what?—a couple months old by then."

Sitting up in surprise, Max cleared his throat. He didn't think he should be hearing this and shifted around in his seat while he scrambled for an excuse to leave. Pappy was drunk and babbling about family secrets Max didn't need to know about.

Or did he? If he wanted to marry Helene, shouldn't he know about her? If he wanted to marry her and start a family, what would it hurt to find out some facts from Pappy? Unintentionally given though they might be.

Pappy didn't seem to register Max's concern. He rocked back and forth in the chair, taking a sip of hooch every sentence or so.

"Yeah, we thought Doris would make it out of high school before she got married, but it didn't happen. I didn't care, mind you." Pappy paused and pointed at Max. "I loved her no matter what. But Grammy, well, she had some definite feelings on the subject. Having a shotgun wedding did not meet with her expectations, no-sir-ee."

Relieved he wasn't coming to Pappy with that issue, Max thought it best to make his request and get home before Pappy passed out from the alcohol.

"You know, sir—"

Pappy picked up the gun and patted it.

"Sorry, sir. I mean Pappy."

The old man placed the gun back down on the table and rocked again.

"Pappy, I have something I've been wanting to ask you. I'm not sure Helene would want me to, but I think it is the right thing to do." Max took Pappy's nod as a sign to continue his question. "You see, I've always wondered—"

The old man interrupted him. "Wondered why she lives with us? Yep, that's a story Grammy wants to take to her grave. But you're a nice young man, and you've got a right to know what yer gittin' yerself mixed up in."

Max stiffened. He'd never considered he was getting mixed up in anything, so Pappy's words seemed ominous. If he didn't speak up, he might learn something that would change his mind about the girl of his dreams. But if she was the one, nothing should change his mind.

So Max sat on the porch and listened to Pappy tell him about Helene's sixth birthday and how she never went back home.

"Helene's daddy was a drinker. I don't know if it was gettin' married so young or bein' a daddy when he was still a kid himself. Maybe Doris pushed his buttons too. God knows she was a handful. I loved her to pieces, but I admit we coulda done a better job raisin' 'er." Pappy sipped his drink and stared out into the dark sky. "Anyways, I shoulda known things was bad when Doris started askin' for money. It wadn't much to start, so I gave it to 'er. Havin' a baby is expensive, so didn't think much of it. Turns out, Glenn drank all their money." Pappy raised his glass and chuckled. "Probably stupid of me to sit here and have a glass while I'm tellin' a story like this."

Feeling out of his depth, Max shook his head. "No, sir. I mean Pappy. One drink now and then doesn't seem so bad."

Max heard the rocking chair creak while Pappy took another sip. He put his glass down on the table before he continued.

"You remember that, son. But be careful. Maybe Glenn thought that's all it was too. By the time we figured out what was goin' on, it was too late. Spent his money. He'd lost his job. Man was a mean drunk. Took it out on Doris. She swore he never laid a finger on Helene, but," he shrugged, "no way of knowin' for sure. Doris wouldn't talk about it. Talked even less after Grammy checked her out of the hospital one night. Said she tripped and hit her head, but I think she covered for 'im."

Sitting up, Max asked, "Where was Helene when that happened?"

"With us. The baby stayed with us once we figured out what was happenin'. Only she wasn't a baby anymore, and it was hard to keep her from hearin' things. She came home with us after her birthday party." Pappy's teeth shown in the moonlight as he smiled. "Mad as a hornet that the clown couldn't come home with us but fell asleep as soon as we got in the car. Next thing you know, we got a call there'd been an accident. Glenn and Doris went to the bar to continue the party. Friend o' mine saw 'em there. Told me Glenn could barely walk when they left. Never made it home."

Pappy stopped talking, and the sounds of crickets chirping and a frog croaking filled the air. Max didn't know what to say about the story and still couldn't figure out why Pappy told him now.

"What does this have to do with Helene and me?"

"Son, you're gettin' ready to ask my granddaughter's hand in marriage, are ya not?"

Surprised at Pappy's astuteness, Max nodded.

"Then you need to know what yer gettin' into. Helene don't know what happened to her parents. She might put it together someday or someone might tell her. And you need to be there for her when she finds out. Make sure she knows this wadn't her fault."

Max frowned. "Why haven't you told her?"

Shaking his head, Pappy said, "I promised my wife I wouldn't. Dumbest promise I made. But a promise is a promise, especially to yer wife." He pointed a finger at Max. "You best remember that. No matter what happens, a promise is a promise."

MAX SMOOTHED Helene's hair as he finished the story. He waited a few minutes for her tears to dry before putting his finger under her chin and tilting her face toward his.

"I must look terrible," she said through a stuffy nose. "My eyes feel all puffy, and my nose has to be red from the crying."

She struggled to turn away, but Max held her close to him.

"You are beautiful. As beautiful as the day we met. And now you know that nothing anyone can do is going to change my opinion." Max saw her lips tremble, but he continued. "You are not your parents. Nothing that happened to you was your fault. Did your grandmother deal with her issues? No. Should I have told you what I knew?" He shrugged. "Maybe. But I do know you have worked harder in the last couple weeks to figure out what makes you tick than you ever have before. There are six weeks before Tasha's wedding, but I can tell you right now that I'm not going to leave your side. I love you, and if you'll have me, I want to be your husband for the rest of our lives."

"If I'll have you? I've been a horrible person to you. I'm so sorry I didn't see it at the time."

"You did what you thought you needed to do. I don't understand it, but Dr. Austen helped me reconcile with it and move past it." Max paused and asked the question he'd been dreading. "The only question now is, can *you* move past it?"

He held his breath as he waited for Helene's response. Dr. Austen had warned him that it might take years before his wife could get over this childhood trauma because she'd kept it locked inside for so many years. All he could do was support her. The rest of it was up to her.

When he saw her smile at him, his jaw unclenched.

"I can't make any promises, but with you and Dr. Austen on my side, I think I can." Helene picked up her list. "I need to get started, though. If it's okay with you, I want to invite the girls for dinner tonight and talk to them both. Are you okay keeping Blake and Libby busy while we talk?"

Max smiled back. "Absolutely. I'm happy to help you."

30

The rest of the morning flew by. Helene still found it hard to believe Max had forgiven her, but she wasn't about to look a gift horse in the mouth. After she had convinced him to take a nap in preparation for the grandkids later that evening, Helene freshened up and started in on the rest of her un-do list.

Next on the list was to invite Tasha and Sara to dinner, which turned out to be harder than she expected.

"Mom, it's a school night. Can't we do dinner on Sunday like usual?" Tasha asked.

Calling on all the patience she had, Helene said as calmly as she could, "I'd like to have Sara join us before she returns to Chicago on Saturday."

There was a longer silence than Helene thought necessary before Tasha spoke.

"Have you talked to Sara?"

Helene circled *Call Sara* on her un-do list. "No, she didn't answer my call earlier, but I'll try again after we're finished." Helene sat up straight when a thought came to her. "Is she standing there? Put her on and I can ask her now."

Another pause met her request.

"Mom, Sara left this morning."

Helene didn't know if the emotion she felt was anger, sadness, or embarrassment, but it triggered a reaction.

"Why would she—" Helene stopped midsentence. Even if Tasha knew what was going on, it wasn't fair to ask her. Dr. Austen had been clear on the fact that Helene needed to treat her daughters as individuals and as adults. If Helene wanted to know what was going on, then she needed to speak to Sara herself. "I'm sorry. This isn't your issue. I'll call Sara. But I would really like it if you could come to dinner tonight. We need to talk, and I think it's best that we do it face-to-face."

She heard panic in Tasha's voice when her daughter asked, "Did something else happen to Dad? You should lead with important medical information, you know."

Helene shook her head. "No, he's fine. He's on track to make the bowling tournament in a couple weeks." She swallowed hard and hoped she wouldn't have to apologize over the phone. Dr. Austen had said it was important she do this in person. "We can eat dinner early so you can be home with plenty of time for the bedtime routine. I promise."

For a second, Helene didn't think Tasha was going to agree. Helene started to offer to drive over to her daughter's house when Tasha said, "Okay. But we're out at 7:45. No questions asked."

With a smile on her face and in her heart, Helene said, "That's perfect. I'll have dinner ready by six, so if you want to come a little earlier, we can talk before dinner."

"Mom, you're making me nervous. You're not usually so agreeable. What's going on?"

Reassuring Tasha that everything was fine, Helene confirmed the dinner menu and let her daughter go.

Before she lost her nerve, Helene dialed Sara's office

number. She'd never called it before, but when Sara moved to Chicago, Helene had programmed it into her phone.

"The Miller Agency. How may I direct your call?" the voice asked.

"Sara Shaw, please."

"Ms. Shaw is unavailable right now. I can take a message or send you to her voicemail."

Knowing Sara might never listen to a voicemail from her, she chose to leave a message. The message taker's surprise when Helene gave her name left no doubt in Helene's mind that Sara had already briefed the office staff on what phone calls to screen. Helene hung up the phone, not expecting to hear back from her daughter.

It served her right. She had spent years meddling in Sara's life and not being supportive of her eldest daughter. She acted like Grammy, but she expected different results. What was that saying? *Insanity is doing the same thing over and over and expecting a different result.* Then maybe she needed to try something else. Or *someone* else as the case may be.

Helene rubbed her temples as she looked down at the next name on her list: Betty.

Despite the fact that Betty had shown up at the hospital when Helene needed her, that didn't mean Betty had forgiven her for lying about how she treated Sara. Helene might not be able to apologize to Sara right now, but Betty should be at the Coffee Bar at this very moment. Maybe if she hurried, Helene could catch her before the lunch rush.

She hesitated. Leaving Max alone wasn't ideal, but at least now she knew what was bothering him. Helene scribbled a quick note to Max in case he woke up, grabbed her purse, and headed out of the house before she could talk herself out of it.

31

On her way to the Coffee Bar, Helene decided it might help grease the wheels a bit if she bought some sides and dessert at Betty's. That way, if Betty didn't accept her apology, it wasn't a wasted trip. Betty would make some money, and Blake and Libby would get their favorite dessert. Even as she thought about the plan, Dr. Austen's voice rang in her head, "Stop manipulating people, Helene. Don't assume there has to be something in it for you."

"Old habits die hard," she mumbled to herself as she parked the car. Helene gathered her bag and stepped out of the car, realizing she hadn't changed out of her jeans. Denim served its purpose, but she steered away from it in public. She had an image to uphold, after all.

"The old Helene had an image. Aren't you trying to be more approachable?" Helene reminded herself. Smoothing down her hair, she ignored the discomfort she felt from not being dressed in her usual fashion and headed into the building. "Besides, who really notices these things, anyway?"

As she opened the door, the familiar sights and sounds soothed her. Betty stood behind the counter waiting on a customer to make her selection. A group of women sat in the corner, gossiping while they sipped tea and munched on what looked like almond pastries. The smell of cookies fresh out of the oven enticed Helene as she took her place in line, for once content to wait patiently.

"Mrs. Shaw, is that you?"

Helene glanced up to see Cynthia from the newspaper staring at her.

"Hello, Cynthia. Yes, it's me. How are you today?"

She kept her expression neutral as she watched the reporter. The girl's face seemed frozen in shock, as if she'd seen something that didn't make sense. Helene followed her gaze. Cynthia's green eyes stared at Helene's feet, taking in the loafers, then worked their way up to her jeans, then to her long-sleeve T-shirt and, finally, to her hair, which Helene self-consciously smoothed again. Apparently, people *did* notice what other people were wearing.

"Cynthia," Helene said, "can I help you with something?"

Cynthia blanched, and Helene bit the inside of her mouth to keep from smiling. The poor girl couldn't believe what she was seeing.

"Um. Yeah. Well, I was . . . going to ask . . . if you were sure about not doing the 'Wedding of the Year' feature." She pulled her eyes off Helene's clothes and focused on her face. Or maybe her head, because Helene could see Cynthia's eyes darting around as if she were counting all the hairs that were out of place. Normally, Helene would pull out her silk handkerchief and corral her head, but today it didn't bother her.

"Yes. Quite certain. No need to include Tasha. She wants a quiet and personal wedding, and I'm happy to oblige."

"Since when have you been happy to do anything?" Eveline Gerome asked.

Helene turned around and saw that Eveline was in line with an empty teacup. She must have been in the corner, but Helene hadn't seen her. "And what on God's green earth are you wearing? You look like a hillbilly farmer." Eveline's eyes narrowed and her lips pursed. "No. You look like you did in high school. A poor, dirty orphan."

Eveline's voice carried through the store, and Helene saw everyone's head turn. Even Betty stopped what she was doing, her hand frozen in the air with a chocolate éclair in route to a bag.

She wasn't kidding about making my life hell, Helene thought. *Should I ignore her or point out that her black ballet flats are scuffed?*

Taking the high ground, she said, "Good thing I'm not that girl anymore." Helene caught Betty's eye and noticed the woman winked at her. That was a good sign and enough encouragement for Helene to continue. "I'm wearing functional and comfortable clothes appropriate for my day. Is that a problem?"

Confronted with Helene's pushback, Eveline narrowed her eyes. "No, although the jeans are not flattering on you in the least. There is a point in a woman's life when tight garments are considered inappropriate."

"Excuse me, Mrs. Gerome, but you're wearing yoga pants," Cynthia piped up.

A twitter of laughter came from the back corner of the shop but died as Eveline shot a look that way. She turned back to Cynthia. "How rude. Young people these days don't know when to mind their own business." The teacup rattled as she placed it on the countertop and pointed at Betty. "You're going to lose business if you allow this type of disrespect."

Everyone's eyes were on Eveline as she marched back to the table, grabbed her fake Birkin, and stomped out of the café.

"Good riddance, I say," said Betty as she finished bagging the pastries and rang up the customer. She nodded at Helene's outfit. "Nice jeans."

Helene smiled back at Betty, then turned back to Cynthia as the reporter continued.

"If you or Tasha change your mind, let me know. The contest doesn't close for a while, and we only need a few pictures to run in the paper. I've seen the dress, and I can tell you, it is the best of the lot."

She nodded and shifted uncomfortably when Cynthia turned to pick up her food from the counter. Confident she'd made the right decision about the contest, Helene wondered if she should suggest Tasha enter on her own. If Tasha was a shoo-in for the award, what was the harm? Shaking her head, Helene knew second-guessing herself wasn't the right thing to do. She studied the pastry case to keep her mind on safer topics.

When Cynthia finally paid for her food and waved goodbye, Helene stepped up to the counter. Betty leaned on the back counter and crossed her arms.

"I told you I wasn't going to serve you again until you apologized."

"So you aren't going to make this easy?"

Betty grinned. "Nope. Too much fun to see you like this, although I'm in a much better mood now that Cynthia said something about those yoga pants."

"I should have bought Cynthia's cup of coffee as a thank you."

"Pay for it now and I'll be sure she gets the next one on you."

Rather than responding, Helene walked around the counter. She held out her arms to give her friend a hug, but Betty stopped her.

"What's this? You trying to steal my fresh cinnamon rolls?"

Laughing, Helene pulled her friend into an embrace. She didn't realize how nervous she was until she felt Betty's arms envelope her. Only then did she relax fully. Helene spoke quietly in Betty's ear, aware everyone in the store was watching and listening to them.

"I'm sorry. You were right that I wasn't treating the girls correctly, and you were a lifesaver at the hospital. Thank you for sticking by me even though I haven't been the friend you deserved." She swallowed hard before she said, "I can't promise to be perfect and never make another mistake, but I can promise that, from here on out, I will listen to you. And to Max. So when I start acting stupid, can you let me know?"

Betty squeezed her tighter before she said, "It would be my pleasure to tell you when you are being an ass. And yes, your apology is accepted."

The women stepped away from each other, and Betty returned to her place behind the counter.

"Now that that's settled, what can I get you?"

Helene relaxed, knowing she and Betty were on solid ground again. "Tasha and the kids are coming over tonight. Some sides for dinner and something chocolate for dessert would be great."

Betty grabbed a pastry box and added a variety of cookies and brownies while Helene scanned the options for side dishes. Her preferred options of German potato salad and artichoke-salami surprise weren't there, but rather than complain, Helene settled on the coleslaw and pasta salad. She started to tell Betty her order, but her friend pulled out two containers from the side of the refrigerated case.

"Don't let this go to your head, but I've got your favorite German potato salad and the artichoke-salami surprise for you. I've been setting some aside every day in hopes you'd come to your senses and apologize."

Tears welled up in Helene's eyes, and she bit her lip to keep from crying. "Thank you. You didn't have to do that, but I'm honored you have faith in me. Especially when I'm still not so sure about things myself." She darted in and gave Betty another hug. After paying for her food, Helene waved goodbye to Betty and headed for the door.

As she was leaving, Helene saw the ladies at the corner table looking at her. After a quick glance at Betty, who gave her the thumbs-up sign, Helene waved to the table. "I'm sorry I've been such a pain in the rear all these years. Feel free to tell everyone!"

A weight lifted off Helene's shoulders, one she didn't know was there, and she hurried out to her car, eager to tell Max about her conversation with Betty.

32

Tasha stretched before she glanced at the clock. Sara should be back in Chicago by now, and the school bus wouldn't drop off Blake and Libby for a few more minutes. That gave her enough time to find out if Sara knew what was going on with their parents. She grabbed her phone and walked to her bedroom.

Her mother's phone call this morning had worried her. Tasha considered calling her dad to make sure he was feeling okay, but she knew her mother was hovering at his bedside. Ever since he'd come home from the hospital, Helene had been overprotective of Max. Sara had mentioned a weird text Helene sent her, asking where Max was when she left the house. As much as she appreciated the fact that Helene had consented to counseling, Tasha was beginning to wonder if her mother had another screw loose.

Tasha dialed her sister's office number. A midweek dinner at her parents' house wasn't unheard of, but she and the kids had visited on Tuesday. Helene hadn't even acknowledged that when she called. Plus, why didn't her mother know Sara had left town?

She didn't have time to consider the possibilities because Sara answered.

"I've only been gone eight hours. Did I forget something at your house, or do you miss me already?"

Smiling at her sister's question, Tasha said, "When was the last time you forgot something?"

Sara laughed. "I am human, you know. Once in a while, I make mistakes."

Tasha sat down on her bed. "Okay. I'll take your word for it. I'm calling because of Mom." When Sara didn't immediately respond, Tasha continued. "She invited both of us to dinner tonight. I surprised her when I told her you went back to Chicago."

"I neglected to tell her I was leaving today. Sorry you had to do that. Did she make a fuss?"

Shaking her head, Tasha said, "No. She didn't."

"That's progress, I guess. Usually, she'd get all upset and ask you to find out what's wrong." Sara paused. "Wait. Is that why you're calling? Because you and I both know you shouldn't be the middleman. If Mom wants to talk to me, she can call me. Not that I'm taking her calls—of which I have gotten three already today."

Closing her eyes, Tasha lay back on the bed before she continued. "Got it. And no, that's not why I'm calling. I'm more interested to see if you know why Mom would want to talk to both of us face-to-face. I asked if something else happened to Dad, but, according to her, he's fine. What else could it be?"

"No clue. Maybe she's doing some sort of twelve-step program with the counselor and she's reached the point where she has to apologize for the pain her actions have caused." Her sister cleared her throat. "Wait a minute. Maybe I do know what she's calling about. Are you sitting down?"

Tasha opened her eyes and stared up at the ceiling. "Close enough. Hit me."

"You know when I stayed with Dad while Mom went to her therapist appointment?"

Massaging her temple, Tasha nodded. "Yeah. I had a PTO meeting. You could have knocked me over with a feather when I found out Mom asked you to help."

"Surprised me too, but Dad needed me," Sara said. Her sister hesitated before continuing. "Promise me you won't be mad."

Tasha sat up and frowned. "Why?"

A long sigh met her question before Sara said, "When I was there, Dad asked me to get some books out of the closet for him. They were in the guest closet."

Tasha frowned. "So? What does that have to do with me?"

"While I was in the closet, I noticed some dresses."

Tasha's heart sped up. She knew she didn't want to hear anymore, but she couldn't help herself. "Let me guess. Wedding dresses."

"Yeah. About a dozen of the same one. I'm guessing it was the dress you originally picked. Mom must have scooped up all the extras she could find when she heard it was discontinued. It left you with no choice but to buy the one she liked."

Squeezing her eyes closed, Tasha took several deep breaths. She'd seen her sister do this before. Something about oxygen regulating people's emotions. After five attempts, Tasha wasn't sure she was any calmer, but she forced herself to speak.

"Don't you think you should have mentioned this before you left?"

"Tasha, I'm sorry. I didn't want to upset you."

Tasha could hear something scrape in the background, and she visualized her sister standing up and doing some sort of yoga stretch while they talked on the phone.

"You're so happy with the dress you got, so I wasn't sure I should tell you. Plus, it makes it look like I'm trying to get Mom in trouble."

"She's good at doing that herself."

"That's what Jared said."

The comment distracted her. "Now that's interesting. You told me things were strictly professional with you and Jared."

"Stay on topic, please. I'm telling you what happened."

Making a mental note to return to the topic of Jared, Tasha asked, "Did you ask Dad about it? He would know what was going on."

"He sent me to the closet. Why would he do that if he knew about the dresses?"

Flopping back onto the bed, Tasha visualized her wedding dress waiting for her at the Wedding Barn, and her heart rate slowed. The thought of it relaxed her, and she felt calm. Sitting up, Tasha said, "I don't care. I love that dress. I look good in that dress. That dress was made for me."

"Exactly!" Tasha pulled the phone from her ear at Sara's exclamation. "She did this on purpose."

Tasha closed her eyes at the thought of her mother interfering in the wedding dress purchase. On one hand, it was a sneaky thing to do, and she needed to put her foot down. On the other hand, she *really* loved the dress. Knowing Sara was watching out for her best interest, Tasha sighed. There had to be a way to deal with her mother *and* keep the dress.

"You're not giving up that dress, are you?" Sara asked.

"No. I'm not," said Tasha, then added, "but I am going to talk to Mom about boundaries. I thought we were on the same page, but obviously we are not."

"Didn't you tell me she brought you cake samples and a crown?"

"That's been dealt with. I ordered the donuts for the reception, and Darci at the Wedding Barn found me a spectacular veil." The thought of the veil made her smile. "I feel a little like Princess Diana."

Sara snorted. "I hope not. She wore a crown with her veil. And she was killed largely because of the paparazzi."

Recognizing her sister's skepticism, Tasha said, "I'm not wearing a crown, and there are no paparazzi in Glen Valley. I'll explain this to Mom tonight at dinner. You know, I should be mad at you for not telling me about this."

"You're right. I should have. Bad judgment call on my part."

Tasha started to agree, but she heard the front door slam open, followed by Blake and Libby's raised voices. As usual, an argument was in process.

"Got to go referee kids. I'll call you when I get home tonight."

"Good luck," said Sara. "And I really am sorry for not telling you about the dresses sooner."

She said goodbye, already over her irritation with Sara. Tasha hoped she could forgive her mother as easily.

33

Helene fussed with the table. "Do you think I went overboard?" she asked Max. "Is the crystal too much?"

Her daughter and grandchildren came for dinner all the time, but tonight was important. Helene needed to make sure Tasha knew she was on the straight and narrow these days. No more meddling. No more controlling things. And she had to confess to the dresses and give Tasha the opportunity to wear the one she originally wanted, even if it was the least fashionable thing this side of the Mississippi.

Her body relaxed when Max's hands rested on her shoulders. She leaned back into him, enjoying the calm and warmth he brought into her life. Then she noticed a fork out of place and tensed. Max must have felt it too because his grip on her shoulders tightened slightly, and he wouldn't let her go.

"Considering we're having barbecue delivered, I'd say you may be a little formal. Plus, you swore Blake wasn't allowed to use the fine china until he was eighteen. He broke a dinner plate last Thanksgiving, didn't he?"

She cringed at the memory of picking up shards of china from the table. "You're right. I need to put out paper plates."

She struggled out of Max's grasp, but her husband spun her around, and all thoughts of the table vanished when his lips pressed down on hers. Without realizing it, her hands wound around Max's neck and she kissed him back, lost in the moment.

It wasn't until she heard giggles that she knew they were no longer alone. They had an audience.

"That's gross, Grandma. Kissing gets you cooties!" Blake said before he ran to the back door. "I'm gonna play outside."

"I want the rope swing!" Libby called after her brother as he disappeared. "It's my turn!"

Helene felt Max squeeze her shoulders as he gave her another quick peck. "I'll go monitor. I can hear the delivery guy outside too." Before he left the room, he gave Tasha a hug. "Thank you for bringing them by. You and your mother can chat before we eat."

The high from Max's kiss dimmed as she turned to face her daughter, who had crossed her arms over her chest.

"Well, well, well. Getting a little action before dinner," said Tasha. "I like your style."

"Natasha! That is no way to speak to your mother!"

Tasha laughed away the admonishment as Helene found herself enveloped in her daughter's arms. Confused, Helene hugged Tasha back. It felt good to have her baby in her arms again. Maybe bittersweet, since her daughter may never speak to her again after she confessed about the dresses, but Helene enjoyed the hug for what it was worth.

"I'm only kidding, Mom, although I am glad to see you and Dad are back on good terms. I take it the therapy is working." Tasha pulled out a chair and sat down. She tapped the plate. "I see you've gotten over the damage Blake inflicted at Thanksgiving."

"Actually, I haven't," said Helene. Nervous about what she needed to tell Tasha, she decided to confess and work at the same time. "Can you help me pick these up? I'm going to put out paper plates instead."

"Good idea," Tasha said as she began stacking the plates.

The two of them worked in companionable silence to unset the table. Once the china was safe and sound in the cabinet, Helene handed Tasha the paper plates she'd brought out from the pantry.

"Here. Put these on the table. I'll be right back." She picked up the crystal goblets she'd put on the table and went into the kitchen to exchange them for plastic drinking cups. The wine glasses she'd placed on the counter earlier caught her eye, and she decided a glass of wine while she confessed was a good idea. Grabbing the bottle of chardonnay from the fridge, Helene rummaged around in the kitchen drawer for the corkscrew.

"All finished. And you're getting started." Tasha leaned on the counter as Helene opened the wine. "Need any help with that?"

"No, I've got it. Do you want a glass?"

Tasha shook her head. "I'm driving. Plus, I don't like chardonnay, remember?"

The corked popped out of the wine as Helene realized what she'd done. "I'm sorry. I do know that. I don't know what I was thinking." She poured herself a glass of wine and frowned. "I can open another bottle if you want. Your father can drive you home, or you can all stay here tonight and go home before school." Helene panicked. This wasn't a good start to her apology. She stared at the glass and wondered if she should pour it out instead.

"Mom, go ahead and drink it. I'm giving you a hard time."

Reassured by Tasha's behavior, Helene smiled. "Thank you. I've been looking forward to this all day." Helene took a sip of wine as Tasha moved to the kitchen table and settled into a chair. "Very good. Can't beat the oak in a chardonnay, can you?"

"I suppose," said Tasha. "So, while you drink that, do you want to tell me about all the dresses in the guest room closet?"

Wine spewed from Helene's mouth sprinkler style, covering the counter, cabinet, and floor around her and sending Tasha into a flurry of laughter. Helene grabbed a towel from the counter and mopped up the mess.

"It's not that funny," she said when Tasha continued to cackle.

Holding onto her stomach, Tasha shook her head. "Actually, it is. I wish you could have seen your face. It was the best thing ever!"

"What's the best thing ever?" Blake asked as he ran into the kitchen. "Dinner's here! Can we eat? I'm starving."

Libby frowned when she saw Helene mopping up the mess. "Do you need help, Grandma? I'm an excellent cleaner. I have plenty of practice cleaning up after *him*," she said as she pulled another towel from a drawer. "Your pants are too pretty to get dirty."

Max entered the room carrying two bags and stopped short when he saw Helene and Libby.

"What is going on?"

"Grandma's cleanin' up a mess and Libby's helpin' her," Blake said. He went to Max and pulled his sleeve. "Can we eat now? I'm really hungry!"

Not wanting to wait until after dinner to finish the conversation with Tasha, Helene looked at Max with what she hoped was a panicked expression he would understand. Max blinked twice, nodded, and headed toward the dining room.

"Come on, you two. Let's get dinner started while your mom helps Grandma."

"I'll take over, Libby," Tasha said, taking the towel from her daughter. "Wash your hands, then go with Grandpa."

"Okay, but that stuff is really sticky...."

Helene helped Libby wash her hands before handing her the side dishes from Betty's.

"Can you take these to Grandpa? We'll be right there."

Helene watched as Libby carried the salads into the dining room, then turned back to the wine on the floor. "Libby's right. The floor is a mess. I should probably mop."

"You can do that later." Tasha held out her hand, and Helene surrendered the dirty towel. "Should I assume from your chardonnay fountain that my question surprised you?"

Helene got off the ground and went to the sink to wash her hands.

"Yes, but not for the reason you think. You're not going to believe this, but I planned to tell you about the dresses tonight. That's why I invited both you and Sara." Helene scrubbed her hands, rinsed them, and dried them slowly before she turned back to face her daughter. She steeled herself for Tasha's reaction. "Your original dress selection is in the closet. If you want to wear the dress to the wedding, I understand. It was your first pick, and I never should have done what I did."

Tasha's right eyebrow arched. "What exactly have you done?"

Taking a deep breath, Helene said, "When you told me the wedding dress you wanted had been discontinued, I spent a couple days on the phone and bought every single dress I could find. They're all in the closet in the guest room." She twisted her wedding ring as she continued. "It was an off-the-rack dress that didn't complement you, and I thought you could do better. I missed out on being able to help you pick a wedding dress when you married Doug, so I wanted to be involved this time around. I should have told you, and I didn't. But the whole reason I invited you to dinner was so I could explain what happened and apologize. I am sorry. I never should have interfered. Your dad told me I was wrong to do it. I shouldn't have pushed you on the wedding crown and the cakes or submitted your name to *The Gazette* for the 'Wedding of the Year' contest."

Tasha opened her mouth to speak, but Helene rushed on.

"Don't be mad at your father about the dresses. He didn't know until yesterday when Sara found them. She did the right thing telling you. But it's my fault, and I'm sorry, and I understand now that I never should've tried to control you, because I never wanted to be controlled. I finally made peace with the fact that my entire life wasn't what I wanted it to be, and I didn't know how to fix it until Dr. Austen helped me see I didn't kill Grammy. Grammy and Pappy did the best they could for me. But I know I'm responsible for my own actions now. I'm so sorry."

Out of breath, Helene stopped and waited for Tasha's reaction. Her daughter's forehead crunched down like an accordion. Her eyes resembled those of a deer caught in headlights, and her mouth formed a perfect O, but no sound came out. For a second, Helene wondered if the information was too much for her daughter, but then Tasha nodded.

"Do you think you can go over that again? Only slower this time?"

34

After dinner, the kids begged Max to play a board game with them.

"I want to be green," said Blake as he pulled his grandfather toward the living room.

"You always get green." Libby crossed her arms and glared at her mother. "Mommy, tell him it's my turn to be green. He can be yellow."

"I don't wanna be yellow! That's a girl color."

"There's no such thing as—"

"Enough." Max took the grandchildren by the hands. "Come on, kids. We'll go work this out. Let your mom and grandma talk."

Helene motioned Tasha to the kitchen table as Max escorted the kids out of the room.

"He always was good with children. Probably better than I was." She sat down at the table and looked over at Tasha. The surprised expression on her daughter's face made her ask, "What's wrong?"

"You did okay, too, Mom. Don't be so hard on yourself."

"Interesting response considering I butted into your

wedding and purposefully prevented you from getting the wedding dress of your dreams."

Shaking her head, Tasha sat down next to her mother. "I have the dress of my dreams now. That dress from Wedding Barn is perfect. No way I'm giving it up, so you can do whatever you want with the dresses you hijacked."

"I didn't hijack them. That makes me sound like a criminal."

"Mom, you confessed to coercing me into buying the wedding dress you picked out. You entered me in a wedding contest without my knowledge and—"

"I withdrew you from that. Cynthia agreed."

Waving her hands in the air, Tasha said, "Let's focus here. Most importantly, you also told me about your parents for the first time. And while I have a lot of questions, at least now I have some inkling of what you went through growing up and why everything has to be your way now."

Helene bristled. "If you're going to pity me—"

"Mother, stop it. This is me understanding you." Tasha took her hand and squeezed. "Why didn't you tell us any of this before? Life would have been so much easier if we'd known."

Helene squeezed back. "We wouldn't be in the same place if I'd explained. I'm sorry for not being honest with you before. I had to be honest with *myself* before I could share things with *you*. You have every right to be mad at me. It's going to take a lot of work to make sure I don't revert to my old self again, but I'm going to do it. For you. For Dad. For Sara."

"What about for you?"

Tasha's question stopped Helene. Dr. Austen had told her that change had to come from within. Every single self-help guru in the world said it. But tonight was the first time she really understood it.

Pulling Tasha's hands, Helene rested her head on her daughter's shoulder. "Thank you for understanding," Helene whispered into her ear. "I didn't know if you would. Especially with all the trouble I've caused."

The women sat back in their chairs.

"Really, Doug's been more trouble over the years. You've got a ways to go before you top him!"

Helene burst out laughing. "That does make me feel better."

They sat in companionable silence for a few minutes before they heard yelling from the living room.

"I think the game is about over. We should get going." Tasha started to rise, but Helene put her hand over her daughter's.

"Do you have any advice about Sara? She's not returning my calls." She felt silly for asking for Tasha's help, but for some reason, she felt like her daughter might have the answer to the question. "Is there any chance I can make things right with her?"

Tasha nodded and stood up. "There's always a chance, Mom." Stepping behind Helene, Tasha put her arms around her mother. As she gave her a hug, Tasha whispered in her ear, "But you made a mistake, and the only way to fix it is to ask for forgiveness. You did that today, and I bet you can do it again."

The words filled Helene with hope. She watched Tasha walk to the door of the living room and call out to the kids, "Libby, Blake, clean up. We have to leave!"

Helene sat at the table, considering how to approach Sara.

"Why don't you fly to Chicago to see Sara?" Tasha suggested. "A big gesture like that might make a difference. Plus, you could get a hotel room for a few days and explore. You love the city."

"Do you think she'll agree to see me?"

Tasha shrugged. "Sara is as hard-headed as you are, Mom," she said. "I think chances are high that you won't even make it into the office."

"Am I on a watch list or something at her building?" Helene

frowned. "That makes me sound so much worse than I really am."

"Stop overthinking this and go get a plane ticket."

"If Grandma and Aunt Sara make up, will Aunt Sara want to be maid of honor, Mommy?" Libby asked from the doorway. "Jessica said adults are better for the wedding party. She said kids make things boring."

"Who's Jessica?" asked Helene.

Tasha shook her head. "Friend from school." She leaned in close and muttered, "'Frenemy' is a more accurate term."

Tasha turned toward Libby. Helene stood up and walked to the kitchen counter. She watched as her daughter took her granddaughter's hand and sat her down at the kitchen table. As much as she wanted to help, she understood this was Tasha's job.

"Sweetie, you can be my maid of honor. It doesn't matter what Jessica says."

"But what if Aunt Sara comes to the wedding?" asked Libby. "What then?"

Tasha glanced over at Helene before she added, "I could have two maids of honor."

Libby's eyes lit up. "That sounds like fun! Can Aunt Sara get a red dress too?"

"If she wants to."

The girl chewed on her lip as she considered the option. Helene noticed a gleam in her granddaughter's eye when Libby turned to her and asked, "Can I have a crown? It only seems fair that I get something for having to share the position."

Helene struggled to keep a smile from her face as she waited to hear what Tasha's answer would be.

Nodding, Tasha told her daughter, "I suppose, if you want a crown, you and Grandma can pick it out together."

Libby hugged Tasha. Helene smiled at the sight of her daughter and granddaughter's love. That was something she had never had with her mother or grandmother, but now she had the opportunity to make things better.

Helene felt Libby's arms around her waist, and she looked down.

"Grandma, can I ask you a question?"

Helene returned her hug. "Yes, honey. What is it?"

Libby paused before asking, "Did Aunt Sara move to Chicago because you set her up with the relationship coordinator?"

"Who told you that?" Helene resisted asking Tasha if she had said it.

"My teacher told the principal at lunch. They think we can't hear them, but we can. Mrs. Anderson's daughter talked to the same relationship person Aunt Sara used before she moved. Mrs. Anderson said that was the reason Aunt Sara left town. The principal said you were a busybody who didn't know when to keep her nose in her own business. Is that true, Grandma?"

Sad that her behavior had impacted Libby, Helene gave a sad grin and caressed her granddaughter's face. "I interfered in things I shouldn't have," she explained. "I wasn't respectful of Aunt Sara."

Libby frowned. "It wasn't very nice of the principal to call you a busybody. They're always telling us to be nice to each other."

"You are absolutely right, Libby," said Tasha. "You should treat people the way you want to be treated."

Once again, Helene understood how much her actions impacted others, in ways she hadn't planned. If only she'd figured it out sooner, she wouldn't be having to explain things to her granddaughter. There was a bright side, though. She was doing the right thing now.

"This shows why it is so important to be nice to people and to admit when you're wrong," Helene continued. "All of this could have been avoided if I had been more respectful to Aunt

Sara. It's because of me that Aunt Sara doesn't want to come to the wedding."

"It's okay, Grandma. I bet if we tell her she can be maid of honor with me, she'll come."

Helene glanced at her daughter for confirmation. When Tasha nodded, Helene said, "Well, I'd better get on that, then!"

35

"Thank you for seeing me on such short notice, Dr. Austen." Helene's foot twitched, and she twisted her hands as she sat on the therapist's couch on Monday afternoon. "I couldn't wait until Wednesday."

Dr. Austen nodded. "So you said when you called." She tapped her pen against her chin. "Tell me how your un-do list is going."

Helene reached into her bag and pulled out her notebook. Placing it on her lap, she flipped it open to her list before she ran her hands down her slacks and straightened to her full height.

"I've accomplished quite a bit. Tasha knows everything and forgives me. Betty accepted my apology. I haven't felt this close to Max in years. I may have gone a bit overboard, but I'm determined to do this right. I treated people in ways I never wanted to be treated." Stopping at one name, she added, "I added the security guard at Max's office. His lack of fashion sense was a favorite stomping ground of mine over the years. As a way of making peace, I got him a new brown belt to wear with his black shoes anytime he wants."

The therapist's lips curved up, making Helene pause.

"Did I say something funny? Or is that coming off as rude? Because I don't want it to be. I am being sincere, but if I'm missing the point, please tell me. I seem to miss a lot of things."

Dr. Austen shook her head. "It's okay to contact people, but be forewarned that not everyone may be as receptive as you want them to be."

Helene looked down at Sara's name. She'd highlighted it in bright yellow. Her daughter had not responded to any of the fifteen voicemails she'd left, which was why she needed Dr. Austen's help.

Before she could tell the therapist her concern, Dr. Austen said, "I take it there's someone on your list who falls in that category."

Helene let out a sigh of relief, then confessed how her relationship with Sara was at a standstill. "Calling her isn't helping. Tasha suggested I go to Chicago. It would be hard for Sara not to listen to me then."

Helene wasn't surprised by Dr. Austen's response.

"It also might make things worse."

"Max said the same thing. He encouraged me to reach out to you." Helene gestured at the list in her lap. "Everyone else I talked to was receptive. Even if they thought I was having a mental breakdown. The cake lady asked me if I'd been visited by aliens."

Helene heard Dr. Austen laugh and glanced up. The therapist cleared her throat before restoring a neutral expression to her face. "Sorry. People's reactions to change always amaze me. There are some people who can't understand that people can change all on their own. They think it has to be made by some external force. Like aliens."

"Is that why Sara won't take my calls?" blurted out Helene. She struggled to maintain her calm. The last thing she wanted to do was cry again, but the thought that her daughter had given up on her made her so sad that she didn't know what else to do. "Am I a lost cause?"

Dr. Austen leaned forward. "I can't answer that question. You'll have to figure it out for yourself. I can tell you that you've made significant progress in understanding how you got to this point. From what I can see, you are putting in the work. But you can't make someone feel a certain way or do what you want them to do. You've tried that before, and how did it turn out for you?"

Helene's shoulders caved forward. "You're saying Sara might never accept my apology, and I have to accept that because it was my actions that caused the rift in the first place."

The therapist nodded. "That's the worst-case scenario, yes. Life doesn't have any guarantees. You know that as well as I do. But given enough time and space, your daughter might come around. It might be tomorrow or next month or ten years from now. Or maybe never. But if you keep pushing her, she's going to keep moving away from you."

It wasn't the news she wanted to hear, but Dr. Austen was right. It was time to let Sara live her own life. But, at the same time, her mistakes impacted Tasha as well. Helene leaned forward.

"I understand I've approached this poorly. My actions created a big gap in my relationship with Sara. But what I don't want to happen is for Sara to miss her sister's wedding because of me."

"Have you told her that?" Dr. Austen asked.

"She won't return my calls or messages."

"So you've said. But have you explained in your messages exactly what you want her to know? That you want her to come to Tasha's wedding?"

"No. Only that she needs to call me back."

"She doesn't need to do anything, Helene," Dr. Austen chastised.

"I know, I know. I got frustrated and panicked, which made the problem worse. Sara shouldn't miss Tasha's wedding because of me. It isn't fair to either one of them. I want to make things better, but it results in me mucking things up even more." Helene dropped her notebook on the couch before standing up and pacing Dr. Austen's office. "Should *I* not go to the wedding? Max could let Sara know that she could attend without having to worry about running into me."

"How would that make Tasha feel?"

Helene turned at the door and walked back toward the couch. "Maybe Tasha doesn't want me at the wedding either."

"You told me Tasha forgave you. Helene, can you sit down, please? The pacing makes it hard to talk to you."

"I'm sorry. I can't seem to do anything right today." Helene plopped down on the couch and put her face into her hands, not bothering to worry about whatever wrinkles she might cause from her actions. "I want to make things right with the girls. It's my fault everything's a mess in the first place, but every time I try to fix something, I make it worse."

Helene felt something touch her arm and looked up. Dr. Austen held out a box of tissues, which made Helene smile.

"I think I'm all cried out, but thanks for the offer."

"That's progress." Dr. Austen put the box on the table and leaned back in her chair. "Is your name on the un-do list?" The question caught Helene by surprise. Before she could think of what to say, the therapist continued. "Or your mother and father?"

She didn't have an answer for how to apologize to herself, let alone how to forgive people who'd been dead for years.

"How exactly am I supposed to do that? A séance? I don't consider myself terribly religious, but that seems a little out there, don't you think?"

The therapist's smile persisted. "No, I was thinking more

along the lines of visiting your parents. Traditionally, flowers are left on gravesites. Have you ever done that?"

An image of a bouquet of yellow roses filled Helene's mind, and she swore she smelled lemons. Shutting her eyes, a picture formed around the flowers. Two caskets, side by side, with a blanket of yellow roses on one of them, the other bare. People stood around, talking softly, while Grammy sat in a rickety folding chair right in front of the flower-covered box. Pappy stood behind her, his hand on her shoulder, but no one else came near them. It was like there was an invisible line drawn around them that no one could cross.

"Helene? Are you okay?"

Her eyes fluttered open, the smell of lemons faint but still present. "No, I've never been back to my parents' graves."

"Why not?"

Waving a hand in front of her face, hoping to disperse the citrus smell, Helene looked at the ground as she answered. "Because Grammy said I shouldn't go there. She always said looking back was a waste of time. So why bother?"

She couldn't bring herself to look up at the therapist, but for the first time this session, the silence felt uncomfortable. Helene brushed away a tear that rolled down her cheek. "Apparently, there are still tears to be shed," she said to herself. The box of tissues reappeared in her line of sight. "Thank you. I don't know why I'm crying again."

"You're crying because you're owed an apology too. Let me make myself clear. You do not owe your parents an apology. There isn't any way that will happen, séance or otherwise. So the next best thing is to go to them. Sit next to their final resting place. Think about what you want them to know about your life. I'm not going to get into a discussion about afterlife and whether their souls have been watching over you, but I will posit that being in the proximity of them will give you something to think about. It can give you closure."

Dabbing her eyes, Helene said, "I was six years old the last time I saw my parents. What am I going to say to them?"

"What do you need to say?"

Helene considered the therapist's question. As she started to speak, Dr. Austen put up her hand.

"You don't need to tell me. Tell *them*. Then you can let me know how you feel."

36

The next day, Helene found herself driving down an unfamiliar dirt road. As she avoided the gigantic washboard rut that ran down the center, she decided calling this a road was an overstatement. It was more like a trail, surrounded by gnarled trees towering on both sides, their branches reaching out over the road, creating a canopy. Leaves blocked out some of the sun, which made it challenging to avoid the greenish, brain-like hedge apples that littered the lane.

Helene cringed at the scraping sound of her car bottoming out in one of the ruts. She glanced at the hand-drawn map sitting in the passenger seat. The cemetery was close. The man at the gas station had said to turn left at the burned-out farmhouse and right at the oak tree that had been struck by lightning. What she wouldn't give right now for GPS. But, of course, the final resting place of her parents would be out in the middle of nowhere with no cell service.

"This is ridiculous. How could I have made a wrong turn?" Helene mumbled to herself as she scanned the sides of the road for the entrance. "And even if I am on the right road, visiting dead people isn't going to solve a thing."

A loud thump made her jump, and she glanced in the rearview mirror to see what she had hit. The remains of several hedge apples coated the dirt road. "Disgusting. Another reason not to live in the country."

Two turns and three more smashed hedge apples later, Helene sighed in relief when she saw an opening on the right side of the road. She slowed down in time to see a small limestone sign with the words "Lone Horse Cemetery" etched in it. This was the place.

Relieved she'd made it to her destination, she turned onto the narrow path and followed it for another fifty yards. The trees surrounding this path closed together, blocking out so much light that it seemed like dusk. When she'd had enough of the path and the dark, the trail dumped her into a large parking lot full of sun. A limestone wall divided the lot from the cemetery. A rusted, wrought-iron gate towered in front of her, and she headed toward it.

It seemed big enough to drive through, but it was closed. She parked the car and got out. Dust puffed up with every step she took, so she tiptoed to the gate. Several sneezes later, Helene concluded she wasn't going to be able to enter the cemetery. The rusted padlock adorning the gate appeared to be at least fifty years old, and she doubted it even worked anymore.

Turning back to the car, Helene said, "Wonderful. Now what do I do?"

Helene jumped when she heard a voice call out, "You could use the side gate."

She scanned back and forth to figure out where the voice came from. She didn't locate its owner, but she did notice a path going off from the parking lot and a sign that said "Entrance."

As she walked back to the car, she called out, "Thank you."

"Anytime," came the response.

Please tell me I'm not talking with the dead. She grabbed the bouquets she'd brought with her. She clicked the lock button on her key fob, and the familiar dinging noise sounded.

"No one's gonna steal yer car out here, lady. Everyone's either dead or has their own."

Someone laughed, and Helene hesitated. Someone was making fun of her. With Dr. Austen's help, she'd gotten better at accepting other people's opinions, but standing in a cemetery in the middle of nowhere without cell service was not the most reassuring place to be. Max knew where she was, but he wouldn't know she was having a problem for a few hours. For the umpteenth time, she questioned her decision to come here alone.

"You comin' in or just gonna stand there all day long?" the voice called out. "Cuz yer gonna need help findin' whoever it is yer lookin' fer, and my lunch break starts in ten minutes."

Helene marched down the path and followed the sign. Sure enough, a smaller wrought-iron gate appeared a few yards from the path. She pushed the gate open and jumped when it slammed shut behind her.

"Auto-closin' hinges. Got tired of closing the damn thing myself." The voice's owner sat on a stone bench under a tall oak tree. Helene bit her lip to keep from calling out in surprise at the man's appearance. His overalls covered a faded flannel shirt that boasted the cemetery's logo on the left side and the title "Caretaker" on the right. A cowboy hat sat on top of his head, its crown dented in and splattered with mud. A scuffed cowboy boot swung impatiently, and his hand rested on a cane that Helene guessed was handmade. His sun-worn face sported wrinkles and age spots that disguised the man's exact age. A little gruff, but harmless. "You ready? Yer down to eight minutes."

Slightly embarrassed for being caught staring, she looked down at the bouquets in her hands and inhaled the sweet smell of the yellow roses. She relaxed and said, "I'm looking for my parents. Doris and—"

"Glenn Nevill?"

Helene wondered if the expression on the man's face matched her own. "Yes. That's them. Do you know where I can find them?"

The man grabbed the cane and pushed himself into a standing position.

"Back this way. I'll take ya." He pushed his crumpled hat off his brow and stared at her with eyes that had seen at least eighty years of sights. Helene guessed him to be about her parents' age, which would explain why he knew who they were. The man gave her a quick bow and said, "You must be little Helene. Never thought I'd see ya here."

Helene felt her eyes widen in surprise. "How do you know who I am? And who are you?"

Plopping the hat back on his head, he tapped his shirt. "This here says I'm the caretaker. It's my business to know who people are. Besides, you look like yer daddy." Without waiting for a response, he turned and hobbled down the dirt pathway. Calling over his shoulder, he said, "Now, let me get ya where ya wanna go."

Helene hesitated. She had come all this way to see her parents, but now that she was here, her nerves threatened to overwhelm her. Shaking off her feelings, she followed him as they strolled along for a few minutes, then turned left and meandered through headstones and monuments and trees and flowers. Some of the graves were old and crumbling, while others appeared to have been recently installed. She wanted to ask the caretaker how he knew her father, but the words wouldn't come.

The man stopped and pointed his cane to the corner of the cemetery. "There's your parents."

Helene took in the stone bench placed under a tall oak tree. A neat hedge surrounded the area. It looked calm and peaceful. She paused, waiting to see if she would feel any different being less than thirty yards from her parents' final resting place. A breeze sent her hair flying in front of her eyes, and the chirping of birds provided soothing background music, but other than that, she felt the same as when she'd walked in the cemetery gate.

"Ya know, you're lucky."

The caretaker's words startled her, and she turned to face him.

"How so?" She couldn't think of anything lucky about standing in a cemetery.

"That area got cleaned up last week. It ain't a priority since nobody visits."

Nodding, Helene asked, "When was the last time someone came out here?"

The man tilted his head to the side and gave her a long look. When she had given up expecting his answer, he said, "Believe it was the day they were buried." With that, he turned and hobbled back down the path. "I'll be eatin' my lunch by the mausoleum if you need anything."

Nervous to address her parents' graves, Helene called out, "Thank you for helping me, Mister . . . ," she said. When he didn't offer his name, she added, "You know, you never did tell me your name."

Without turning around, he called out, "Nope, I didn't. Say hi to your mother for me," and continued his trek to the mausoleum.

Unsure what to do with the knowledge that she was the first and only visitor to her parents' gravesite, Helene let out a sigh and made her way to the bench. She held the bouquets of flowers in front of her like a shield of sorts. It wasn't much use, since her hands were shaking the closer she got to the bench.

Helene stepped through the opening in the hedge and saw the two gravestones. Moving closer, she examined them.

Her father's marker was small and simple. It listed his name, birthday, and the day he died. The dull surface looked out of place next to her mother's stone. Doris Parker Nevill's stone was four times larger than her husband's. The polished surface shined up at her as if it were brand new. Along with her birthday and death date, the stone boasted an inscription and a drawing of a rose in each corner. Helene stepped closer to read the inscription.

I couldn't protect you. But I will watch over you.

Helene bent down and placed one bouquet of yellow roses on her mother's final resting place. She started to put the other arrangement on her father's grave, but something stopped her. She turned and sat on the bench, holding the flowers in front of her.

Closing her eyes, Helene listened to the sounds around her. In addition to the birds she'd heard earlier, the rustling of leaves made crackling sounds. Nothing but nature met her ears. Although she knew her parents couldn't hear anything, Helene thought this was the perfect place to spend eternity.

She was stalling, so she opened her eyes and looked around. Clearing her throat, she hoped the caretaker was far enough away that he wouldn't hear her as she muddled her way through what she needed to say.

"Hi. Mother. Father. Or Mom. Dad." She shook her head. "I don't even know to call you, it's been so long. I hear you don't get many visitors. Myself included. Grammy told me not to come here."

Helene stared down at the bouquet, stroking a petal on one of the flowers.

"She held a grudge. Against the two of you. And against me.

It's taken me a while to figure that out." She laughed before she continued. "Actually, it took me almost losing my husband before I understood."

Max's face popped into her head. He had wanted to come with her this morning, but she'd convinced him she needed to do it alone.

"I think you'd like Max. He put up with me for years, and when he couldn't deal with it anymore, he found me help. He didn't leave me like he could have. It's okay to ask for help, by the way. I learned that too. And forgiveness."

Her ignored phone calls to Sara reminded her that forgiveness wasn't guaranteed, just like so many things in life. She looked at her mother's headstone and wondered what Doris would think about how she'd lived her life.

"I've been working with a therapist."

She put the roses on the bench, then nodded at her father's name.

"You probably wouldn't approve of that, but I'm doing it. Dr. Austen, my therapist, helped me understand I have some forgiving to do. That's actually why I'm here today. You can't answer me, but I'm going to tell you anyway. You see, Dr. Austen helped me understand that death is final. Irreversible. At least for now." Helene chuckled. "It's amazing what types of medical advances have been made in the last few decades."

Her face saddened as she continued.

"Even though there isn't anything I can do about the past, I've decided I want a different future. The two of you can't take back what happened or how I grew up."

Helene's voice hitched as she thought of how her father's choice had altered the course of her own life forever. But if he had made a different decision, she might not have found Max. Her life would have been entirely different. Even though she'd made a mess of her relationship with Sara, she wouldn't trade it for anything. She still had Max and Tasha and Blake and Libby and Betty. And hope that maybe, someday, Sara would return her calls.

Clearing her throat, she continued.

"I spent years feeling guilty, thinking it was somehow my fault. Grammy didn't help matters. It made her feel better to blame me. Dr. Austen helped me understand I didn't do anything wrong. At least not when I was a child. I've done a lot of things wrong as an adult, but Dr. Austen helped me figure out how to change that.

"The point I'm trying to make is that this"—Helene pointed at the cemetery around her—"wasn't my fault. I don't need to feel guilty about it."

She picked up the roses before she continued.

"I'm making changes while I still can. For instance, I'm making amends for the mistakes I've made, and I'm moving forward. My younger daughter Tasha and I are on good terms. She's getting married again. Don't get me started on the first husband. That was a train wreck, but I like Greg. He's a keeper. Good to Tasha and the kids. That's right. You have two great-grandchildren, Blake and Libby."

Helene paused. It wasn't like her parents actually heard her, but even thinking about Sara hurt.

"I have another daughter. Sara. She's an attorney. Brilliant woman. Single. Just moved to Chicago. Sara's not speaking to me at the moment. I'm working on that. I don't know if I can fix things there, though. I made a mess."

The breeze picked up, and the lemony scent of the roses hit her nose. She relaxed and let the aroma wash over her. Things were peaceful here. More than she ever imagined. Making up her mind, Helene decided she would take the peacefulness as a sign that she could make things right with her daughter. If a trip to the cemetery could mend her feelings toward her parents, maybe a trip to Chicago would prove to her daughter how much she'd changed.

Helene stood up and placed the bouquet of roses on her father's headstone.

"These are for you. I won't be back, but I wanted to say thank you for bringing me into this world. I've got a lot to be thankful for, and I couldn't have done it without the two of you." She adjusted the bouquet on her mother's headstone and frowned when she remembered the caretaker's request. "By the way, the caretaker said to say hello. He seemed to know both of you, though he wasn't inclined to tell me his name. Too bad you can't tell me."

Taking one last look at her parents' headstones, Helene retraced her steps to the parking lot. The peace she had felt at her parents' side continued, and not even the caretaker's appearance near the side gate altered it.

"Will ya be back anytime soon?" he asked as he leaned on his cane.

Helene passed by him and shook her head. "No. I said what needed to be said. Thank you for your help today. The place is beautiful." She stopped in front of the gate. "Can you tell me your name?"

The man smiled and pointed at his shirt. "I'm the caretaker."

Nodding, she pushed the gate open and walked to her car. She was anxious to get home and tell Max about her day and her decision to visit Sara.

37

Sara pushed back from her desk and raised her arms over her head. She leaned from side to side, enjoying the relaxing sensation that came from the stretches as well as the knowledge that she was finally caught up. Her trip to Glen Valley the week before had been important. She had wanted to see her dad and help out while he was recovering. At the same time, she had a job to do. Playing catch-up the last few days was a necessary evil.

She settled back into her seat when she heard a knock on the door.

"Come in," she called, a smile already forming on her face. Jared had started dropping in more often since she'd gotten back as well. Apparently, absence made the heart grow fonder. If you believed that sort of thing.

The door swung open, and Jared waltzed into the room with two cups in his hand. "Ready for your daily dose of caffeine?"

He closed the door behind him and made his way straight for Sara's desk. After he set down the cups, he took her face in his hands. She wasn't sure if her cheeks warmed up because of anticipation or Jared's touch, but she forgot what she was thinking when he leaned down and pressed his lips onto hers.

A few seconds later, she disengaged her lips. "You know, if we keep this up, someone is going to catch us. Isn't there a no dating policy in the employee handbook?"

Jared gave her one final peck on the cheek before he picked up his coffee and returned to the other side of her desk, settling himself into one of her side chairs.

"I removed that policy. Sometimes it's nice to be the boss." He took a sip of his coffee and nodded at the desk. "Are you at a stopping point?"

The cup of coffee stopped on its way to her mouth. "Why? What do you have in mind?"

His gaze met hers. "While I like where your mind is headed, the motivation behind this coffee is to make sure you're in a good mood before I tell you who's in the lobby."

Sara's eyes narrowed as she glared at him. "God. Whatever it is must be bad if I got a kiss and coffee." She took another sip before she said, "Brianna is sitting out there, isn't she?"

Jared stretched out his legs in front of him and shook his head. "Not Brianna."

Sara relaxed a bit. "That's good to know. I'm still not sure I'm ready for another encounter with her."

"You won last time. The hair-pulling was exceptional."

Her cheeks warmed again as she remembered the fight she'd had with Brianna back in her office in Glen Valley. Not one of her finer moments.

"True, but not something I want to repeat." Frowning, she asked, "Is it Doug?"

Jared grinned. "After my last exchange with your ex-brother-in-law, I don't expect to see him again. Ever."

Her cup stopped midway to her lips. "Michael Seaton?"

He shook his head again. "Nope. No one has heard from him since we confirmed his contract was invalid." He put his cup down on her desk and leaned forward. "Enough guessing. Your mother is here."

For a second, Sara froze. Helene was the last person she imagined would drop in. Especially since a visit in involved a plane ride and a rental car, and her father was still recovering. At the thought of her father, she straightened.

"Did something happen to my dad?"

He smiled at her and shook his head. "He's fine. Helene said he's been cleared to bowl. Tonight is the league championships, and he's anchoring the lineup."

"Sounds like you had quite the conversation with my mother."

Jared leaned back in his chair and smiled. For a second, Sara forgot about the fact that her mother was sitting in the lobby waiting to ambush her for some unknown reason and let herself take in Jared's exceptionally good looks. She felt hot and tingly. Then she remembered her mother, and everything went cold.

"What if I don't want to talk to her?" asked Sara in her best attorney's voice. "Maybe I have something else I need to be doing."

The smile on Jared's face brightened. "I wondered what you'd say. Especially since she told me you've ignored all fifteen of her voicemail messages."

"Sixteen, but who's counting?" said Sara, standing up. "It won't end well."

Jared stood up and walked around the desk. Putting his hands on her arms, he pulled her close. "I don't know what is going on, and it is none of my business—"

"You're absolutely right."

Smiling down at her, Jared continued, "You should talk to

her. Or at least listen. For no other reason than to make sure she understands your position and ends this now. If you don't, she'll continue to call you. Give her a chance to explain so you both can move on. I wouldn't ask if I didn't think it was important."

She'd shared a lot with Jared since they started dating, but this was the first time he'd pushed her on any personal matters. This was a big request, and a serious one at that. Sara chewed on her lip. She couldn't believe her mother would talk to someone she barely knew about their relationship. Something was up.

"I should call Tasha," Sara said, pulling away from Jared to reach for the phone.

Jared pulled her back toward him and, before she could complain, placed his lips back on hers. All thoughts of calling her sister faded as her eyes fluttered closed and she felt his soft lips caress hers. As soon as she relaxed, Jared pulled back.

"So, can I send in your mom now?"

"Please don't tell me she put you up to this." Sara walked back to her desk and pulled a mirror and lipstick from the drawer. She reapplied the color to her lips before looking at Jared. "Because if she did, and you complied, I've got issues."

He laughed as he picked up his coffee. "Nope. This was all my idea. I thought you might be more receptive if you were in the right frame of mind." As he let himself out of her office, he called over his shoulder, "You've got sixty seconds to straighten up your office."

Shaking her head, Sara knew he was teasing her. Probably for a good reason too. He wanted her mind off the conversation that she was going to be having with her mother.

"I think this is as clean as it gets." She waved her hand over her desk. Other than the stack of papers on one side, her computer, and her "World's Best Aunt" mug, her desk was clear. "Send her in. I'm as ready as I'll ever be."

Her stomach quivered at the smile Jared gave her.

"You'll do fine. Give her a chance. You might be surprised."

She watched him leave the room, then sat down. Having a significant other was great until he convinced you to talk to the one person you'd moved hundreds of miles to escape.

With a sigh, Sara leaned back in her chair and waited.

38

Helene twisted her wedding ring while she waited for Jared to return. There was a strong possibility Sara would refuse to see her, but Jared had assured her that he would do the best he could to help. She wasn't sure why Jared was so accommodating. Tasha or Max might have called ahead to give him an idea what was happening. That made the most sense.

She paused. The thought of Tasha or Max intervening on her part didn't bother her as much as she thought it would. In fact, it didn't bother her at all. She didn't need to worry about accepting help from others after all.

Jared walked back into the lobby, a smile on his face and a coffee cup in his hand.

"Are you ready?" he asked.

Not trusting her voice, she nodded.

"Are you sure I can't get you some coffee before you go in? It might calm your nerves a bit."

She stopped messing with her ring and stood up. "I'll be fine. Point me in the right direction."

Jared held out his elbow. "Let me escort you."

She took his elbow and let him lead the way down the hallway. She caught a glimpse of the Chicago skyline through a conference room and gasped.

"You okay?" Jared asked.

Tearing her eyes from the sight in front of her, she glanced at him and discovered his blue eyes staring at her under his concerned brow. She smiled and patted his hand. "Yes, I always wanted to see Chicago like that," she said as she pointed at the view. "It took me by surprise."

Instead of continuing down the hallway, Jared turned them both into the empty conference room and stopped in front of the floor-to-ceiling glass. "Take your time. Get a good look. Sara will understand."

Helene shook her head. "I don't want to keep her waiting. That would be rude." She bit her lip to keep from smiling at the irony of her statement. She routinely made Sara wait because she knew how much it irritated her daughter. "We can head back to her office."

As she turned away from the window, she jumped when she saw Sara standing in the doorway.

"Hello. I'm sorry. The view distracted me." Helene stepped toward her daughter. "Lead the way to your office."

"That's okay," said Sara. Helene couldn't make out the expression on her daughter's face, but what she said next was more confusing. "Jared's right. Take a minute." Sara walked into the room and sat down at the conference room table. "We can talk in here if you want."

"I'll leave you two alone, then," said Jared. He offered his hand to Helene. "It was nice to meet you, Mrs. Shaw. I hope you enjoy your visit."

Helene noticed Jared winked at Sara as he left the room. Her daughter's face flushed, and Sara shook her head slightly.

If she hadn't seen it with her own eyes, Helene wouldn't have believed it. Sara had found a man on her own. Granted, one she was working with, which seemed very un-Sara-like, but it was a man, nonetheless. Sara was capable of looking out for her own love life.

When Sara's gaze returned to her, though, Helene saw what looked like an attorney walking into a trial. Serious and completely professional.

"What can I do for you, Mom? Popping up without notice is one of your typical surprise tactics, but this is stretching it a bit, don't you think?"

Helene licked her lips and nodded. "You are right, but this time my visit isn't for nefarious purposes. Before I say anything else, thank you for seeing me today. You're busy. I've been keeping up with the agency's projects, and I can see you don't slow down at all. Five new renovations in the last six months. That's impressive. Knowing how much you have going on, I won't keep you."

Sara frowned and cocked her head to one side. "You know how many projects I've been working on?"

Nodding, Helene pulled out a chair opposite of her daughter. "I was curious and wanted to know what you'd been doing. You probably won't believe me, but I have missed you."

"Missed giving me a hard time?"

Helene stiffened. She knew this wasn't going to be easy, but Jared's warm welcome had given her hope. Reminding herself to stay patient, Helene said, "No. That's what I'm here to apologize about. I miss seeing you. Your move to Chicago was due to my bad behavior."

"That's more like it." Sara sat back in the chair and crossed her arms. "Giving yourself all the credit. Did it occur to you this might be a good career opportunity as well?"

Helene looked out the window. All she wanted to do was apologize for her behavior, and here she was, making it worse.

She faced her daughter again. "You're right. I am not the

center of the universe. That's something else I need to apologize for. I've made a lot of mistakes."

"Yes, you have," Sara said.

Helene looked down at her hands folded in her lap. "I wish I could take back some of the things I did. But I can't. The best I can do now is apologize for my behavior and show you that I've changed." She looked up and saw the disbelief in her daughter's eyes. "You have every right to think this is just another ploy on my part, but things are different now. Tasha encouraged this visit. Apparently, she knew that if I called you wouldn't answer. But she didn't think you would turn me away if I showed up here. So, I have to thank your sister for that advice."

Her mouth dried up, and she wished she'd accepted Jared's offer of coffee. She had a lot left to tell Sara, and the cotton mouth she was experiencing was going to make it tougher.

Clearing her throat, Helene started again.

"I've interfered with both you and your sister's lives. I justified my actions because I thought I knew what was best for you. Stepping over the line in many cases didn't matter to me because I thought the end result was what mattered. Your feelings didn't. For that, I'm sorry."

Something flickered in her daughter's eyes, but she didn't know what it was. Rather than ask, she forged on.

"I called you hard-hearted before you moved. I don't know if you remember that. It was the day you had to go to the newspaper office to get a retraction, and you stopped by the Coffee Bar to pick up danishes for all the people who showed up complaining in your office."

Sara nodded. "I remember. Pretty hard to forget that day, both because of what you said and what Cynthia printed." She paused before continuing. "You hurt my feelings."

Sorrow filled Helene's heart. Her daughter had never admitted to having feelings, let alone anyone hurting them.

Helene knew her chances at reconciling with Sara had taken a nosedive.

"But you've come too far to give up." Dr. Austen's voice popped into her head. *"Yes, you've been a royal pain in the ass for years. No, your family doesn't have to forgive you. But you do have to try. Regardless of what they say to you or what you feel, you have to make an attempt."*

"I'm sorry. I can't take back what I said before, but please know that, when I said it, I was hurting. My grandmother never thought I was good enough, and I believed her. Which brings me to the next part of my story." Helene paused to gather her strength. What she said might be the most humiliating thing she'd done. "I never talked about my family because I was ashamed. Grammy and Pappy raised me after my parents died—"

"Mom, I know all this," Sara interrupted.

"Let me finish. Please." She wanted to end this conversation now and let Sara think she really did know all of it, but then she would never be truthful to herself or her family. "You don't know all of it. I made a birthday wish the night before my parents' accident. For a long time, I thought it was my fault they died."

Helene flinched when Sara's hands slapped down on the table.

"Mother. That's ridiculous! They died because your father was drunk when he drove into a tree."

Whatever Helene had planned to say next disappeared from her head. "How did you find out?"

"It's a matter of public record. I wouldn't be a good attorney if I didn't know how to research my facts." Sara stood up from the table and walked to the credenza. She opened a cabinet to reveal a mini fridge and pulled out two bottles of water. Walking back, she handed one to her mother and opened the other. "Drink that. You're pale. I don't need you passing out on me about something I already know."

Helene did as she was told and drank half the bottle in three gulps. The shock of discovering that everyone knew about her parents embarrassed her. She'd gone years thinking no one would want her around if they knew about her past, and now her family had proven her wrong.

When she'd gotten herself calmed down, she asked, "How long have you known?"

"Since law school. A criminal law class gave me the idea to research police records."

Frowning at Sara, she asked, "Why didn't you say something to me about it? And why didn't you tell your sister?"

Sara shrugged. "She and I weren't terribly close, if you recall. Plus, she and Doug were having problems by then. It didn't seem fair to add to her misery. It was enough I knew the truth. It made sense why you did what you did, not that it excused some of your more over-the-top schemes. And it didn't make up for the things you said to me."

Helene shook her head. "No, it didn't. I'm sorry. That was the worst thing a mother could say to her daughter. I understand if you can't forgive that, but I wanted you to know that one incident has bothered me so much. I didn't realize how much until I was able to talk to my mom and ask for her—"

"Hold up! Talk to your mom? She's dead." Sara squinted and leaned forward. "You can't talk to dead people, despite what some people say. What kind of therapist did Dad send you to? Because I don't think he got his money's worth."

Helene got out of her seat and walked to the window. Putting her palm flat on the glass, she sighed. "Dr. Austen is great. She sent me down the right path, even if it may be a bit unconventional. Long story short, I had unresolved emotions about killing Grammy and knowing that my father killed my mother."

If she wasn't so nervous, Helene might have laughed at the expression on her daughter's face.

"Back up. Grammy died from a stroke. There is no way you could have caused that."

Helene nodded. "I know that now. But it wasn't until Dr. Austen pointed it out to me that I accepted it. She sent me to the cemetery where my parents are buried to get some closure." She turned from the window back to her daughter. "I know you can't talk to dead people, but it was peaceful. I got some insight, which is part of the reason I'm here now.

"What's important for you to know is that what I did to you and Tasha, and your dad for that matter, wasn't right. I didn't have the right to push my opinions on you all the time and manipulate you to do what I wanted.

"Tasha knows about the wedding dresses I hid." Helene put up a hand to stop Sara from interrupting. "But the interesting thing is she doesn't want the old dress. She likes the one I picked for her. And I'm okay with the fact that that is the only thing she wants my help with. That's how it should have been from the start.

"Both of you are old enough to make your own decisions without me. I'm old enough to know not to interfere." She smiled. "At least I am now.

"I've done a lot of talking. But I want you to know that I am sorry for the pain I've caused you and for whatever role I had in making you move from Glen Valley. I never intended to drive you away, but I did. And I hope you'll be part of Tasha's wedding. I don't want our issues to impact anyone else."

Helene turned back to the window and admired the skyline one more time. Sara's lack of response unsettled her. For once in her life, she had taken responsibility for her mistakes. It was out of her hands now. Taking in a deep breath, she straightened herself to her full height and turned to face her daughter.

The blank expression on Sara's face gave her nothing to go

on, so she resigned herself to wrapping things up. "Thank you for listening to me. I can find my way out."

Sara nodded but didn't make any other movement.

Her heart sinking, Helene knew she needed to keep her word. She gathered her purse and left the room. As she hurried to the lobby, Helene wondered how soon she could get home. There was no reason to stay in Chicago now.

39

"Glad to have you back!"

Max grunted from the force of Frank's pat on the back. He stepped out of the man's reach before he replied, "Good to be here. Doc said I was good as new." Before anyone else could bring it up, Max asked, "How did Greg work out?"

Claude looked up from shining his bowling ball. "Greg's a great guy. Tasha's one lucky lady," he said before he grinned. "But, man, he can't bowl worth a crap! The Geezer Glens are in last place. Our only chance is for you to bowl a perfect game tonight. Even then, we can only place third."

Pete and Frank nodded their agreement.

Max made a mental note not to tell Greg what the guys had said. Despite Betty's recommendation, his soon-to-be-son-in-law had warned him he was rusty, which turned out to be the understatement of the year, since Greg's sub-one-hundred scores put a damper on the Geezers' chances in the tournament. Next time, Max would pay more attention to Greg's self-assessment.

"Best I could do under the circumstances. But I'm back, so let's get going."

Going into the tenth frame, Max's optimism picked up. He'd bowled a perfect game to this point, and he only needed three more strikes for a three hundred. Surprised by his comeback game, he sat down to wait for his turn.

Behind him, several bowlers from other teams congregated to watch the Geezers accomplish the impossible. He overheard several of them muttering.

"They were sandbagging us. Isn't that against the rules?"

"Nah, he really did end up in ICU. My wife works at the hospital."

"Whatever. He probably faked it. He's just like his wife. Helene can't stand losing, so why would her husband?"

Max stiffened. He wasn't sure if the men knew he could hear them or if that was part of a plan to unnerve him. The bowling league was known to be cutthroat.

Before Max could hear any more of the men's comments, Frank sat down next to him and slung his arm around Max's shoulders.

"Great to have you back. I wondered if Helene would let you bowl again. It's good to see who wears the pants in the family."

Someone snorted from behind Max as he pulled out from under Frank's arm.

"I don't appreciate that. Helene and I are partners, and we do what's good for the family."

Frank laughed. "Is that why Helene went behind Tasha's back on the wedding dress?"

The pins in the bowling alley crashed and made a noise, but the only thing Max could hear was Frank's comment.

"Where did you hear that?"

Rubbing some chalk onto his hands, Frank shrugged. "Around. Probably the same place I heard that Helene went out to the cemetery to put her ghosts to rest. That's kinda woo-woo, ain't it?"

Max felt his blood pressure rise, which the doctor had said to avoid and would also be bad for his last frame. But he felt helpless to do anything about it. Helene had done all this, but to hear it told back to him by someone he considered a friend felt hurtful.

"You know, we should focus on bowling. I've got three more strikes to get so we can advance to the next round." He picked up his towel and added, "That's if you can pull your own weight."

The comment hit the mark, and Frank nodded.

"Got it. You don't want to talk about Helene. Makes sense."

Max couldn't help himself. "And why is that?"

Frank smirked. "Because she left you here all alone to fend for yourself while she went to Chicago. Sounds like she's finally getting out of here but not taking you with her."

Throwing his towel into his bowling bag, Max stood up. "I don't know what you're talking about, Frank. She went to visit Sara. Now, if you don't mind, I need to focus to wrap up this game."

Max grabbed his bowling ball off the stand and walked into the lane. Methodically, he went through his wind-up routine. Line up to the left of the center marker, both toes on the line. Deep breath before bringing his lucky blue-and-white bowling ball up in front of his chest. He exhaled and counted to three.

But when he got to three, the time he should have walked four steps while rotating his arm back and gently releasing the ball into the lane, he stopped.

He couldn't believe Frank wanted to gossip at a time like this. And all Claude had done tonight was complain. Pete hadn't been particularly supportive either. It was almost like the team didn't really care if he was here. He was just fodder for their pessimism. He shuddered to think what would happen if he missed this shot.

His shuddering ceased when a bolt of realization flashed through Max's body. He needed to make some changes, just like Helene did. Dr. Austen had told him to stand up to his wife and make sure she understood how he felt about things, but it made sense that he do the same to his friends, or whatever Frank really was.

Max gazed around the bowling alley. The same sounds and sights surrounded him as they had for the last four decades. This was what he'd always wanted. His dad had grown up here, and he thought he would be happy here. He was. But after everything he'd been through with Helene and what Dr. Austen had taught him, now he knew the truth.

This wasn't his dream anymore.

Putting the ball down to his side, Max turned away from the lane and walked away.

"What in the hell are you doing?" Frank asked. "You need to finish your turn."

Shaking his head, Max cleaned off his ball before putting it on the return. "I need a minute. My blood pressure's too high, and I need a break."

"You can't do that," Frank said. "It's against the rules."

Max walked away from the lane. "Bad Boy Ballers took a day off in the middle of their tenth frame last year. Nothing says I can't take a break, get something to drink, and relax before I finish this."

Frank frowned. "Fine. But don't take all night. I want to get this wrapped up so I can call Mike and tell him the Holy Rollers are out of the running for the trophy."

Leaving Frank to gossip with the rest of the team, Max headed toward the bar. He didn't want anything to drink. He needed time to consider his thoughts and regroup before he rolled the last frame. Then he needed to decide what he planned to do.

"Hey, Max. What are you doing over here? Rumor has it you're three strikes from a perfect game." Brad patted Max on the shoulder when he reached the bar. "I don't think you're cleared to have a beer, are you? And you don't drink when you're bowling. Everything okay?"

Max nodded. "Just taking a little walk. Needed to relax for a minute. Blood pressure's acting up, and Helene will be miffed if I end up in the hospital again." Max put out his hand and shook Brad's. "I didn't expect to see you here."

Brad pointed to a table in the corner where Carlton was engrossed in watching lane three. Max followed the chiropractor's gaze and noticed he was studying Tom Clark, the winner of the league's "Worst Bowling Form" trophy for the last five years.

"He wanted to watch one of his patients. The guy comes in every week complaining about how bad his back hurts, so Carlton wanted to see exactly what he does during his game." Brad shook his head. "Personally, I think that's going beyond the call of duty for a chiropractor, but Carlton is determined to get this guy feeling well."

"Good luck with that one."

Max and Brad watched Tom send the ball down the alley, leaving the seven pin behind. The man turned and limped back to his seat.

"How are you feeling?" Brad asked. "Tasha brought the kids over yesterday, and she said you were doing so well that Helene decided to fly to Chicago. Any update on that?"

Glad to have someone who knew the situation, Max said, "She called before I left for the alley. She met with Sara this afternoon. A 'neutral meeting' is what she called it. Sara didn't kick her out of the office, but she also didn't accept her apology. I told Helene to take it for a win and enjoy the rest of her trip.

She took a boat tour, then planned to go to one of the art museums. Someone at her hotel recommended a show where the actors get drunk and recite Shakespeare. I'm not really into Shakespeare, but maybe it would be better that way."

"Well, that sounds like progress. Tasha mentioned she is happy with how things are going with her mom," said Brad. "I have to admit I was surprised to hear about all the things Helene's been meddling with, but the fact that she came clean is pretty amazing." He looked around, as if to make sure no one could hear him. "I know it's none of my business, but Tasha told me about Helene's trip to see her parents. That therapist is brilliant."

Nodding in agreement, Max said, "She's pretty good. Helene's back on track, so that's a good sign." The men stood there, watching Tom roll a gutter ball, when Max remembered something. "Aren't you supposed to be in Chicago this weekend? Helene said you had a meeting with your surrogate."

Max saw Brad's jaw clinch as his eyes dulled over. "We were, but the surrogate backed out...." Brad's voice trailed off.

"I'm sorry. That has to be hard for the two of you," said Max. A cheer from the other end of the bowling alley reminded Max what he was supposed to be doing. "Hey, I don't mean to cut this short, but I should get back to my lane and finish the game. When Helene gets back in town, the two of you should come over for dinner."

Brad nodded with a sad smile on his face. "We'd like that. Good luck tonight!" Without waiting for a response, Brad turned and walked back to the table where Carlton sat. Max watched as Brad said something to his partner, who looked up with a smile and waved. Max waved back before heading back to his lane.

As he passed the other teams, Max made a mental note to ask Helene when they could schedule dinner before he focused back on his game. The brief rest gave him time to prepare. He stepped up to his lane in time to see Frank, Claude, and Pete giving each other high fives.

"What's going on?" Max asked as he joined the men.

"Bad Boy Ballers choked!" Claude did a fist pump. "We clinched third place, even if you don't to hit a single pin."

Frank frowned. "But we can snag second place if you roll at least one more strike. Can you do it?"

Max picked up his bowling ball and stepped up to the lane. "You bet I can."

40

"I don't know why you needed me here, dear," Helene called from the armchair in the lobby of Darci's Wedding Barn. Her daughter and granddaughter had disappeared a few moments earlier, but not before getting her settled out front. "The final fitting is in a few weeks."

Tasha's muffled voice wafted from the fitting room. "I need your expertise, Mom. You told me to ask if I wanted your help, and I do."

Helene still couldn't believe Tasha had forgiven her. The confession and apology from two weeks ago had changed how the mother and daughter interacted. Helene stayed out of Tasha's way, but Tasha called her more often and included her in things that she normally wouldn't.

Last night's donut tasting was the perfect example. She'd had a spectacular time sampling the different donuts and getting to see firsthand a sample of the glamorous donut hole cake Tasha had selected. Who knew that raspberry-glazed donut holes would make an elegant cake? And a portion-controlled one at that.

Things would be perfect except for the fact that Sara had

yet to contact her. Helene had hoped her trip would show Sara things were different now and that she could come home for her sister's wedding, but she'd heard nothing from her daughter since that day in the office. Guilt and frustration put her on edge, but she'd done all she could do. If she continued to pester her daughter, she'd be back where she was—an overbearing, irritating mother.

"Have a glass of champagne," Darci said. "Tasha brought a bottle as well as some appetizers. From the looks of things, you may be out here for a while."

"Is everything okay?" Helene wanted to go back to the fitting room to help, but she knew this was her rightful place. "There shouldn't be much left to do to the dress other than make sure the bustle works."

Darci put a champagne glass in Helene's hand, then placed a plate of cheese, meats, and crackers on the coffee table in front of her.

"Everything is fine. Relax and enjoy. The girls are having fun primping. They've prepared a runway show for you."

Helene gestured to the chair next to her. "Do you want to join me, then? It feels strange sitting here without someone to talk to."

Shaking her head, Darci said, "I've got to run back to check on them. One of my assistants is helping, but I told Tasha I'd be right back. She wanted to make sure you were comfortable."

She watched Darci walk through to the fitting rooms before glancing at the drink in her hand. Max insisted he drive her to the store, so he must have been told ahead of time what was going on. Rather than worry about it, she took a sip of the champagne and relaxed into her chair. The bubbles tickled her nose and went straight to her head. She selected a slice of cheese and put it on a cracker before adding a thin slice of salami.

"Oh, what the hell," and popped the entire thing into her

mouth. Her mother-of-the bride dress was a little loose after her weeks of worrying, so a few extra carbs wouldn't make a difference.

As she enjoyed the small snack, she reflected on the changes in her life. She and Max were in a better place. In fact, they were closer now than they had been in high school.

Dr. Austen was the key to everything, though. If Max hadn't forced Helene to see the therapist, she wouldn't have seen how her insecurities and guilt had clouded her relationships. She might still be fighting with Tasha over what kind of wedding cake to serve and forcing her daughter to comply with *The Gazette's* "Wedding of the Year" contest guidelines.

Thinking about *The Gazette*, she smiled at the opportunity Cynthia had given her. Cynthia wanted her to write a how-to column on wedding planning for the newspaper.

"We can't pay you anything, but the material you put together for the contest was more complete than anything I've seen before. You could write a weekly article on each subject in the application. You could even highlight some local businesses, getting them some coverage for free."

"Why would you offer this to me?" Helene had asked.

"Honestly, I wish my mother was more like you."

Never before had that comment been uttered about her. She was the mother no one really wanted. But all that had changed, thanks to Dr. Austen.

A soundtrack of processional music filled the lobby, and Helene looked toward the fitting room doorway. Darci came through first and sat down next to Helene.

"Tasha's testing out some music while we're at it today. Let me know what you think."

Helene nodded. She preferred a string quartet over the vocal soundtrack that was playing, but this was Tasha's wedding.

When the song got to the chorus, the fitting room door

opened, and Libby waltzed out in her red dress. Helene smiled as she watched her granddaughter twirl and strut around the room. Someone had put her hair up in a bun with a few curls cascading down, the rhinestone crown encircling her hair.

"What do you think, Grandma? Do I look good?"

Helene put her glass on the table, stood up, and gave her granddaughter a hug. "You look perfect!"

Satisfied with the answer, Libby wiggled out of her grandmother's arms. "Okay, I have to go back now and help Mommy and—"

"Libby!" Darci interrupted. "Remember what your mom told you!"

Helene frowned at the wedding store owner's reaction as she watched Libby run back to the fitting room. The door slammed behind her.

"What did Tasha tell her?" Helene looked over and noticed Darci's face had lost most of its color. "Are you okay?"

Nodding furiously, Darci stood up. "Fine. Just going to run back and see if I can help." She dashed back to the fitting room, leaving Helene alone with the music.

Rather than obsess about the odd behavior she'd witnessed, she took a sip of champagne and settled back in the chair again. Helene grabbed another piece of cheese to munch on while she waited. The song continued, and she heard a murmur of voices come from the other room. Helene almost called out to ask what was taking so long, but remembering her vow to only help when asked, she closed her eyes and listened to the music.

She couldn't make sense of the lyrics, but the melody relaxed her into a calm state. She couldn't remember spending a day where she hadn't coordinated everything. It was nice to enjoy someone else's efforts. And it was nice not to be fighting with anyone. The need to always be in charge brought with it a tension she hadn't noticed until it was gone.

The music changed, and this time she did recognize the song. Sara's favorite song filled the lobby area. Sitting up, Helene opened her eyes and waited. She was curious why Tasha had included her sister's song in her wedding.

The door to the fitting area opened, and Libby came spinning out again. Helene smiled as her granddaughter walked up to the full-length mirror at the back of the lobby. She stood to the side, as if she were practicing for the wedding itself.

"I'm back," Libby waved, "and I knew where to go without anyone telling me!"

"You're a smart one! Good work," Helene said. "What's taking your mom so long?"

Libby smiled and shrugged.

Helene turned to Darci to see if she knew what was going on, but a swirl of something black coming out of the fitting room caught her eye, and she frowned.

"What is going on? That isn't the dress your mother picked."

Before Libby could answer, Sara stepped out into the lobby. Her daughter glided into the room, her hands full of a bouquet of miniature red roses, dressed in a black A-line dress with a sweetheart neck and a delicate lace jacket topping the ensemble.

"What do you think?" Sara asked as she spun around. "Libby said it matched your dress."

At a loss for words, Helene sat there and closed her eyes. Was Sara really standing in front of her, or had she had too much champagne? Forcing her eyes open, Helene smiled as Sara stood in front of her, now with a frown on her face.

"Are you okay, Mom? This was supposed to be a surprise, not a shock."

The music changed again, and Helene recognized the song Tasha had picked for the bridal entrance into the ceremony.

She nodded at Sara, hoping her daughter would understand she was too overcome with emotion to talk.

Sara returned the nod and turned back to stand next to Libby. The two of them watched as Tasha entered the room. Even though Helene had seen the dress many times, the sight of her daughter wearing the beaded veil and carrying the hand-tied bridal bouquet took her breath away.

Helene huddled in the chair, her hands over her mouth to stifle the sobs she couldn't control. Tears fell freely as her body shook with joy.

Libby patted her leg. "Grandma, are you okay? Don't you like Aunt Sara's dress? I didn't mean to spoil the surprise earlier, either."

Taking in a deep breath, Helene blew it out slowly, trying to regain her composure. She pulled several tissues from the box on the table and mopped up the tears on her face. She knew the tears wrecked her makeup, but she didn't care.

"Libby, I'm crying because I'm happy. You didn't do anything wrong. Sara looks lovely. I wasn't expecting to see her. Your surprise worked!"

"Good. She and Mommy made me promise not to tell you anything," Libby said. Helene thought she detected a bit of smugness to Libby's voice, and it was confirmed when Libby continued, "Blake doesn't know about Aunt Sara's visit. Mommy didn't think he could keep a secret."

Darci held out her hand to Libby. "Let's go get you changed so you can have a snack."

This must have been part of the plan as well because, instead of complaining that she wanted to stay with the adults, Libby allowed herself to be led away, back into the fitting room area.

Helene shook her head as her daughters approached. Never had she expected that Sara would be here. It was a miracle of sorts. Each of her daughters extended a hand to her. She took them and let them pull her up.

"You okay?" Tasha asked.

"Fine. Overwhelmed, but fine."

Once she was on her feet, Helene dropped their hands and walked around her girls, studying their dresses, admiring the way her daughters looked. She knew they were waiting for her to say something, but she feared that, if she spoke, she would end up in tears again. She hadn't expected to experience this again. To have the three of them standing together when she thought the relationship with Sara had been damaged forever. This truly was her best memory.

Clearing her throat, Helene said, "I'd like to hug you both, but I don't want to muss your dresses." Turning toward Tasha, she smiled. "I love the veil. That looks amazing. You made the right choice. It looks beautiful on its own."

"Thank you." Tasha leaned in and gave her mother a kiss on the cheek. "I'm going to go back and help Darci with Libby."

As Tasha sashayed back into the fitting area, Helene turned to Sara.

"You look stunning. The dress suits you." She folded her hands together and looked at the floor. "Thank you for coming back to stand up for your sister. I know it means a lot to her."

Sara reached out and took her hand. "I've been thinking about what you said when you came to Chicago. Actually, what you did when you visited."

"I barged in without an appointment and interrupted your day is what I did. Hopefully I didn't cause a problem. That wasn't my intent."

Her daughter shook her head. "No. No problem." She pursed her lips, then said, "It *is* a problem, actually. I thought I understood why you are who you are. And yes, I moved to get away from you. I'm an adult and can make my own decisions.

Maybe they aren't the decisions you would make, but they are mine."

Helene swallowed nervously. Whatever it was Sara planned to say didn't feel like it was going to end on a positive note. But she had promised herself and Dr. Austen that she would face up to the difficult conversations, and she wasn't about to break that promise now.

"Even though I'm making my own decisions, I would still like to be able to bounce them off someone else."

Helene's heart rate ticked up a bit. Was Sara insinuating she wanted to talk to her? Struggling to keep calm, Helene bit her lip to keep from asking the question that popped into her head.

"You're not even going to ask?" Sara said. "I figured you'd jump on this immediately."

Still unsure that she was understanding her daughter correctly, she asked, "Do you mean you want to bounce ideas off *me*?" She shook her head. "I haven't been the best person to offer unbiased advice, remember?"

Sara nodded. "Agreed. But when you came to Chicago, you seemed different. For the first time, it felt like you understood what your past actions meant, and you seemed like you wanted to change. I've talked to Dad and Tasha. Betty even called me. Everyone said you are working on yourself and it's real this time. I don't want to miss out." She raised her free hand, still holding the bouquet. "Don't get me wrong, though. This is not a carte blanche invitation to provide unsolicited advice. But I want to know that, if I need someone to talk to, you'll be there for me." She held the bouquet of roses out to Helene. "Does that work for you?"

Tears pricked at her eyes as she covered her daughter's hand with her own. They held the flowers between them, and Helene bent her head to lean her forehead on Sara's.

"Yes, that works for me. Thank you."

41

"Well, it sounds like you've done plenty of therapy on your own between our sessions," Dr. Austen said with a smile before she added, "in addition to helping Max recuperate."

Helene squeezed Max's hand.

"He's an excellent patient. With lots of patience." A nervous giggle escaped her lips. Ever since Max confessed to knowing about her past, she'd felt free. Not everything was fixed yet, but it was closer to what she'd always hoped for. "The girls and I are making progress. It isn't perfect, but Sara is coming home for Tasha's wedding. She's hosting a shower for her sister, and I'm invited. So, we've got a good thing going right now."

"She's underselling herself, Dr. Austen," Max said. "Sara called her last night to ask for advice on what to serve at the shower. Never thought I'd see the day when Sara and Helene were collaborating on menus."

"It's not me, exactly." Helene blushed at her husband's compliment but knew she needed to give credit where credit was due. "Dr. Austen, you told me that if I would back off and let the girls do their thing, they'd ask when they needed help. And you know what? It works."

Dr. Austen scribbled something in her notebook before asking, "So, how do you feel about your marriage now, Max? When we started, you gave Helene ten weeks to turn things around. We're eight weeks in, and you both look remarkably better than when we started."

Max leaned over and kissed Helene on the cheek. "We're good. Better than we've ever been."

Helene's heart swelled with emotion at Max's words. She thought back to the first time she'd come here. The worry and frustration of what she was feeling had made her assume there was nothing she could do to fix her life. But as Helene had seen over the last few weeks, it was up to her to make things better.

It wasn't just her family, either. Last night's Bunco games were more inviting and comfortable. It had to do with her change of demeanor for sure. She listened instead of dominating the conversation. That particular habit wasn't something she had realized before, but when it had been pointed out to her, she was happy to resolve it.

BY THE END of the night, several women asked her advice about therapy and if she thought it would be good for them. Even Eveline Gerome chimed in.

"Dr. Austen is my therapist too. Why doesn't someone ask *me* about her?"

The fact that Eveline admitted to needing help shocked the group as a whole. Helene pretended to be surprised as well, which turned out to be a good thing.

At the end of the evening, Eveline pulled her aside. "Thank you for not saying anything about seeing me at Dr. Austen's office. I needed to make that announcement myself."

"You're welcome." Helene hadn't known where the conversation was going, so she waited to see if Eveline planned to add anything else.

"I know we haven't been friends through the years. Frankly, you irritated me during high school. The orphan sympathy vote rubbed me the wrong way. Not to mention the fact that Max should have been *my* husband."

Helene hoped the shock of hearing Eveline's confession didn't show on her face. The conversation was awkward enough, and the woman hadn't addressed the fact that they'd been in-laws for a few years.

"And don't get me started on Doug and Tasha's marriage. That was a disaster waiting to happen. And it did, thanks to Doug's lack of integrity."

Startled by Eveline's admission of Doug's guilt, Helene's eyebrows rose, yet she bit her lip to keep from interrupting the woman. The monologue got more interesting as it went.

"He never was a smart man. Not like his brother, anyway. But Brad can't seem to find a good woman to settle down with. If he'd move out of this town, it would help. There are no good women here."

Helene nodded. She didn't plan to be the one to tell Eveline that Brad *had* settled down. That wasn't her place. Certainly not anymore. But she did have something to share.

"Be careful what you wish for, Eveline. Sara moved to Chicago. She's dating someone too, but I miss her desperately."

Eveline waved off Helene's warning. "It's not like we see him much, anyway. He's always working on a project. The model citizen, if you will. Just not the best son. He could stand to be a bit better."

SHAKING her head to clear away the memory of the previous evening, Helene leaned into Max.

"Yes, we are happier than we have ever been. Oh, and did I

mention Max bowled a perfect game in the tournament?" She smiled at her husband. "I couldn't ask for anything more."

Dr. Austen's notebook closed with a snap, and Helene looked at her.

"Why did you shut that? We still have forty-five minutes left in the session."

With a smile, Dr. Austen said, "I think we can call it a day. Actually, we can wrap up the routine therapy as well. If something comes up, give me a call. But right now, you both have an excellent grasp on what to do for each other as well as yourselves. While I'd be happy to take your money for each session, I've got a list of people waiting to get in to see me. Most of them are referrals from the two of you. For that, I need to thank you. As a show of my appreciation, today's session is on the house. I think the two of you should get out of here and use the time to go do something fun together. What do you say?"

Max lifted Helene's hand and kissed it. "Works for me. Helene?"

She leaned in and kissed him. "It's the best idea I've heard all day."

The two of them got up together and turned toward the door. Before Helene left, she turned back to Dr. Austen.

"Can I give you a hug? I feel like you deserve it for putting up with me."

The therapist smiled, placed her notebook on the table, and stood up. "I'd be honored."

As the women embraced, Helene wondered what things would have been like if her mother had lived. Would she be hugging her right now? Would she have needed therapy?

Speculating didn't help. What mattered was where she was right now: on track for the first time in her life with Max by her side. It was the best thing she could ask for.

WANT MORE OF TASHA AND GREG?

Download *My Best Ride* for free

Want to know more about Tasha and Greg's wedding? Curious about what ideas Helene planted? Sign up for Carole's newsletter to receive *My Best Ride*, a hilarious look at the couple's transportation option for arriving at their wedding.

Get *My Best Ride* at www.carolewolfe.com.

ABOUT THE AUTHOR

Carole Wolfe started telling stories in the third grade and hasn't stopped since. While she no longer illustrates her stories with crayon, Carole still uses her words to help readers escape the daily hiccups of life. Her debut novel, *My Best Mistake – Tasha's Story*, follows a single mom as she stumbles through one mishap after another.

When Carole isn't writing, she is a stay-at-home mom to three busy kiddos, a traveling husband and a dog that thinks she is a cat. Carole enjoys running at a leisurely pace, crocheting baby blankets for others and drinking wine when she can find the time. She and her family live in Texas.

Follow Carole at www.carolewolfe.com

- facebook.com/carolewolfeauthor
- twitter.com/CaroleW30064418
- instagram.com/carolewolfeauthor

ALSO BY CAROLE WOLFE

My Best Series

My Best Mistake - Tasha's Story

My Best Decision - Sara's Story

My Best Memory - Helene's Story

Made in United States
Orlando, FL
28 June 2022